A Castle for Dragons

Dragons of Eternity, The First Archive

By: Julie Wetzel

This one is for Jessica
Thank you for everything. Love you Sissy!

A Castle for Dragons
Copyright ©2015 Julie Wetzel
All rights reserved.

ISBN: 978-1-63422-128-3
Cover Design by: Marya Heiman
Typography by: Courtney Nuckels

One

HORROR WASHED THROUGH KATHRYN AS SHE STOOD BY and watched the great, black beast cutting across the sky.

Reports had come back from the outlying farms of a dragon stealing livestock, but no one had really believed them. Dragons were mythical creatures—stories told to scare bad children into being good. And even if they were real, they were long gone from the world. No one believed in dragons anymore, but there it was. A dragon. Big as life, with scales black as night. Something dangled in its claws.

Squinting, Kathryn could just make out the wiggling legs of some farm creature. It wasn't big enough to be a cow, maybe a sheep or pig. Whatever it was, it was someone's precious livestock, gone to fatten up the huge creature that shouldn't have been there.

Kathryn glanced back when she heard a noise

behind her. Turning her attention to the dragon again, she continued to watch the creature in the sky. "Do you see it?" she asked as her father came up behind her.

The older man placed a hand on his daughter's shoulder and looked out over the southern fields. "Yes," he answered, pulling her back from the open space. "Get inside before it sees us."

He turned the girl and pushed her to the safety of the house. Well, relative safety. How safe was a thatch-roofed house when there was a fire-breathing dragon on the loose? Tuning around, he watched the dragon disappear in the direction of the forest before heading into the house himself.

"What are we going to do?" Kathryn asked as she peeked out of the shuttered window in the direction of the field. The dragon appeared to be gone, but just knowing it was out there terrified her.

"You are going to get back to work, girl." Her father came over and pulled her away from the window. He checked to make sure the bar was across the shutters, locking them firmly in place. "Dinner will not make itself."

Kathryn let out a sigh and went to the hearth to check on the pot hanging there. Dinner was well on its way to being done. It was times like this when she wished her mother were still alive. At least then, she would have someone to listen to her concerns.

She glanced at her father. He had gone back to the door and was looking out over the fields. Kathryn truly loved the man, but he hadn't been the same since her mother had drowned in the lake. He'd gotten much more protective of Kathryn. She was no longer allowed to go out without either her brother or her father accompanying her. The man had also turned away several offers for her hand in marriage. Not that she wanted to marry any of the young men who had asked, but for goodness sake, she was nearly twenty. If things kept going as they were, she would end up a spinster.

The sound of hooves announced Kathryn's brother's return.

"Did you see it?" His animated voice echoed through the house as he rushed inside. "It was a dragon. A real, live dragon! Just like Grand's stories. It was huge!" her brother rambled on in excitement.

Kathryn glared at him, irritated. Trever was nearly a grown man. Where did he get off bouncing around like such a child? She would have chided him for such actions if her father weren't there.

"Yes," Kathryn's father said quietly, "we saw it."

"We chased after it, but it disappeared into the woods."

"You shouldn't have been out there chasing after

it," Kathryn reprimanded him. Didn't he realize it was dangerous chasing after a fire-breathing creature? "You could have been killed!"

"I knew what I was doing," Trever scoffed.

Kathryn let out a sigh. Arguing with him would do her no good.

Their father considered both of his children. "Lord Dunham needs to be told about this." He looked at his son. "Trever, come with me and explain what you saw to the lord."

Turning to Kathryn, he gave her a pointed stare. "Stay here, and don't go outside." With that, he led Kathryn's brother out, and the door shut behind them with a resounding thud.

Another long sigh slipped out of Kathryn as she listened to the men get the horses and ride off to the castle. Great. Just another excuse for her father to keep her locked up. *Bloody dragon!*

The hinge on the window creaked as Kathryn peeked out. The shadow of the dragon skimmed across the ground as the great, black beast circled above the town. The chaos of its arrival had ceased as the townsfolk hid in fear. No one here would be able to defend themselves from such a terror. When the dragon first appeared a few weeks ago, Lord Dunham called every able-bodied man up to the castle to train for the fight against the creature, leaving the village vulnerable. Maybe that was what had brought the dragon in from the outlying farms. Maybe it had heard that Lord Dunham was going to start hunting it as soon as the men were trained in the use of the newest weapons.

As it was, the entire town had gone into overdrive, trying to get enough real weaponry to outfit all the men. Even Kathryn had been doing her part. There was no telling where Lord Dunham had come up with so many pieces of plate mail, but the stuff wasn't fitted to any of the men properly—it chafed and cut after just a few hours of use. The women of the village had spent the last few weeks slaving away, trying to weave enough material to make padding for the men. At least the danger had gotten Kathryn out of her home for a while. Her brother and father were both at the castle, training.

The dragon's roar rattled the walls of the village hall. The women huddled in the middle of the room as dust drifted down from the rafters. Kathryn cringed away from the sound but turned to look out the window again. Curiosity ate away at her; she had to know what the dragon was doing out there. Pulling the shutter open just a bit, Kathryn could finally see what was going on.

The great beast had moved from the town to the castle. It flew wide circles around the stone structure as it slowly descended. Obviously, the thing wasn't too bright. Didn't it know there was a whole army of men inside, waiting to take it on?

It was distant, but Kathryn's keen eyes saw movement from the top of the battlements. The men had to be up there, ready to strike at the dragon as soon as it was in range. They didn't have to wait long for their chance. The dragon shifted its wings and dropped down as if it were going to land on the pathway leading to the castle.

The archers didn't give the beast time to finish its landing before they attacked. A rain of arrows fell on the dragon. The creature roared in surprise and pumped its wings, regaining height, but the poor thing wasn't fast enough. A loud *thunk* reached Kathryn's ears right before the dragon roared in pain and tumbled out of the air. While the regular arrows bounced off the creature's shining scales, its hide stood no chance against those new contraptions that threw out heavy arrows with wickedly barbed ends.

Thrashing about on the ground, the dragon righted itself and blasted the wall with fire before throwing itself back into the air. Screams of the men caught in the dragon's flames echoed through the town.

Kathryn's heart clenched as she watched the beast pass overhead and take off towards the south. Grabbing up a bolt of new material, she rushed to the door and threw it open. She wasn't a healer, but it didn't take a genius to bind a wound. Other women joined her in her flight, racing to check on the injured. This was going to be a very long day.

An echoing roar was the only warning the castle had of the dragon's second attack. The thing dropped out of the sky like a rock. Kathryn looked up in terror as the great, black beast landed on the castle wall. When the dragon had come earlier that day, it had seemed smaller from the village. It looked so much bigger now that it was close. The solid stone wall swayed dangerously under the thing's massive weight. Or it could have been the way the beast kept flapping its wings as it held on to its perch. Either way, the wall was not going to stand up to the onslaught for long.

"Move, girl!"

Some man in armor grabbed Kathryn's arm and shoved her towards the open door of the castle. All the women were running inside. The men, on the other hand, had turned to face the creature. Arrows were already in the air as Kathryn ran up the steps and into the main hall. Rushing past the long tables, the women huddled against the inside walls, as far away from the danger as they could get. A horrifying rumble and screams rattled through the castle as the outer wall finally gave way under the dragon's persistence.

Kathryn cringed as the dragon roared. Flames washed over the open door, making the women scream. Thankfully, the fire passed too quickly to catch on anything. More screams of rage and pain mixed with the roar of the dragon as all hell broke out in the bailey. Kathryn closed her eyes and plugged her ears. There was nothing the ladies could do at this moment but wait for the dragon to leave.

After what seemed like forever, a man stumbled in from the courtyard. "It's gone," he said as he dropped to the floor just inside the doorway.

The women rushed to his aid, but Kathryn passed him and went to the open door.

Her feet stopped in pure shock, and tears sprang to her eyes as she surveyed the scene. The outer wall had been knocked over into the bailey, and all the outbuildings were ablaze. The men who were still on their feet were doing their best to pull the injured away from the flames.

Kathryn sniffed back her grief and rushed out to see what she could do. It was hard to turn off the emotions surging through her. She knew these men. They were friends. But right now, they would benefit more from her steady hands than her tears. There would be time enough for tears when the wounded were safe.

A gentle hand settled on Kathryn's shoulder. She looked up to find Eustace standing over her. The town elder's eyes were as red as hers, but his tears were nowhere to be seen.

"Come on, girl." Stooping down, he caught Kathryn under the elbow and urged her up from the dirt. "You need to get some rest."

Kathryn would have laughed in irony if she'd had the heart, but so many had died in the last few days. Her father and brother were both listed among the dead—her father had been crushed when the wall fell in the dragon's second attack, and her brother had been foolish enough to go with Lord Dunham's son to hunt the dragon down. Word had just come back that most of those men had been killed. Shock had stolen the strength from her limbs, and she had collapsed to the ground where she stood. Under Eustace's gentle hands, Kathryn staggered to her feet and let the old man help her into the town hall.

"Why don't you rest here for now?" he said as he laid her on one of the many pallets that had been made up for injured survivors. Sadly, more than one held a girl who had lost her family this week.

Even though she had a nice home on the edge of town, Kathryn lay down without a word. Just like the other girls here, her world had been ripped apart. Again. She lay there, listening to the others cry out their grief, while tears slipped down her face quietly. Turning her face into the bedding, Kathryn let out the sobs she had been working to hold in. She would allow herself this one night to cry, but with the loss of so many, she would have to pull herself together fast. Falling apart was not a luxury she could give herself in this time of tragedy. She knew this pain, but many others did not. Tonight, she would give into her grief. Tomorrow, she would help those who knew nothing of loss.

The roar of the dragon echoed through the town once more. Kathryn rushed out to watch the creature attacking the castle. It was not surprising that the enraged thing came back to finish what it had started. The lord's son had made a terrible mistake in chasing after the creature when his father had been killed. Now they all would pay for it.

Villagers ran for cover as the dragon bathed the castle in fire. The stones blackened under the unrelenting flame, but the inferno was not hot enough to damage them permanently. The heat, however, was enough to drive several from the castle. Ending the fiery onslaught, the creature dropped down into the bailey. Kathryn couldn't believe her eyes when it took to the skies again—dangling in its claws was what could only be a human. The relentless shrieks were those of a young woman. Maybe one of the maids from the castle.

Turning in the air, the dragon dropped and flew low over the village. It let out a roar, shaking everyone to their souls. The poor young woman screamed in fear as the creature carried her away across the field to the southern forest.

Kathryn stared after them in shock. *What could a dragon want with a young girl? If he were going to kill the girl, why carry her away?* Noise behind her made her turn around.

"This creature has to be stopped!" one of the village men yelled. His arm, badly burned in the dragon's second attack, hung in a sling.

"And how do you purpose that we do that?" Eustace asked. "We have no men to fight it." It was obvious the village elder was as upset by the dragon's new behavior as the injured man was.

"There has to be *something* we can do." There was a note of pleading in the man's voice. The hopelessness of their situation was starting to settle in on everyone. So far, the dragon had only attacked the castle, but they were all sure it would not be long before it turned its attention to the town.

Eustace stood, staring off in the direction the dragon had gone. "Maybe there is something we can do." He turned to the injured man. "We can send a message to the king, asking for help, but it will take a few days of hard riding to get to his castle." The village elder raised his voice. "Is anyone up for the trip?"

A few stepped forward, and the healthiest was chosen to take the message to the king. It took no time for the village to pack rations and send the young man off on the best horse that could be found.

Kathryn looked back towards the south. Was it really a good idea to call in help from some unknown king? True, they did need help, but what type of person could stand against a dragon? Hadn't Lord Dunham's attempt proven the creature was unbeatable? Most likely, whomever the king sent would just rile up the beast and get them all killed.

Chapter Two

"You summoned me, My Prince?" Patrick dropped to one knee and bowed his head.

Kyle Mylan, the dragon prince, looked over his oaken desk to the young dragon kneeling on his rug. "Yes." Kyle shuffled through his paperwork, looking for his map. "I have a mission for you."

"Truly?" Patrick looked up at his friend. Finding a way to prove himself had turned into a real challenge since he had risen to the rank of Elite. He had worked hard to gain his status in Eternity, but the world of dragons had been quiet recently. How could one gain a name when there was nothing to do? No wars to fight. No maidens to save. Other than a few territorial arguments, the dragons of the world had done a decent job of keeping their heads down and out of trouble. And no one gained fame for deciding whose sheep had wandered onto neutral ground.

"Truly, my brother," Kyle waved for Patrick to stand and come over to his side, "we have a serious problem."

Patrick's heart lifted as he stood and came over

to look at the maps. A serious problem meant a real possibility to carve out his place in the world.

"Father has received reports of a black dragon plaguing a village just south of here." Kyle pointed to a spot on his map. "Eyewitness accounts tell us that the dragon has ravaged Dunham Castle, and the lord and his family were killed during the attack."

Concern filled Patrick's face. This truly was a problem. The dragons had all taken oaths to remain hidden from mankind. "Have you spoken with the guardian for this area?" He tapped the symbol on the map, marking the home of the dragon charged with monitoring the region.

"No," Kyle shook his head. "She hasn't reported in, so I sent a messenger two days ago, but he has not returned yet."

"Did he fly or ride?" Patrick looked at the map, calculating the distance and time it should take to reach the guardian and return. Two days should have been more than enough if he flew.

"He flew." The note of concern was heavy in Kyle's voice. "I fear he has run into trouble."

"Do you want me to find the messenger?" Patrick asked. This would be an excellent first mission to test his skills.

Kyle shook his head. "No. I've already sent William to search for our missing man."

Patrick nodded. If Kyle didn't want him to go after the missing messenger, what did he want him to do?

The tone of Kyle's voice dropped as he went on. "It's also reported that this dragon has started stealing maidens."

Anger flared in Patrick's heart. "My Lord!" There was nothing else he could say. No words could carry the horror and outrage Patrick felt at this statement. Such a dragon had inspired the persecution of known dragon families long ago. Hundreds of dragons had fled for their lives as mobs burned their homes and killed any they caught. Patrick's family had been one of the first to be captured. He had been spirited away by an old woman whom his father had once saved, but his parents had not been so lucky.

Kyle turned in his chair to face Patrick fully. "We must stop him, Patrick. I want you to take two squadrons to Dunham Castle. Secure the village, find this beast, and bring me his head."

Patrick's mouth fell open. This was a mission for a senior dragon, not one just out of training. "My Prince," he protested, "surely you want someone more experienced for this task."

A smile turned the corners of Kyle's mouth. "I can think of no one better. Besides, as my brother, you should be more than ready for this."

15

"Everyone knows that's a farce," Patrick scoffed. "It's well known that I'm an orphan, and a red dragon to boot."

Kyle gave him a disappointed look. "You were raised by our Queen Mother and carry the name My-lan. You may not be her flesh and blood, but you are her son and my brother. And I *dare* anyone to say otherwise in her presence." He tapped his finger on the table, emphasizing his point.

Patrick smiled at Kyle's protective streak. He had always been there to stand up for Patrick in times of trouble.

"You have trained for this, and there is no one more deserving of this opportunity."

It was true. Patrick had trained harder than the other members of Eternity. He believed in the cause and truly wanted to protect dragons from the possibilities of another purge. "But, why would anyone want to go into battle under me? I've never led troops outside of practice." So many of the other Elites had real-world experiences that Patrick did not.

"Ah," Kyle nodded, seeing Patrick's point, "but there are two sides to this coin."

This made Patrick raise an eyebrow.

"Once the dragon is destroyed, the village of Dunham will need a new lord. You may not know much about battle, but you do have knowledge of running a keep. And if this area is as ravaged as I fear, they will need a man with your experience."

Enlightenment crossed Patrick's face. "And the people of the village would be more likely to accept a leader who vanquished a dragon than a man appointed by the king."

Kyle nodded. "Better a warrior than a courtesan."

"So who will lead the assault on the dragon?" Patrick asked. Surely, Kyle had picked out someone better than he.

That impish smile crept back across Kyle's face. "You will. But, I'm sure Daniel will be happy to help with planning."

A relieved sigh slipped from Patrick. Daniel was well versed in the ways of war. He would be a great asset on this mission. "Very well, My Prince," Patrick said, accepting his assignment. "I shall not fail you in this."

"I know you won't, brother." Kyle reached out and squeezed Patrick's arm reassuringly. "Good luck."

"What a dreadful mess." Daniel sighed as they rode up on what was left of Dunham Castle.

A quick glance had Patrick praying the place was livable. One wall of the battlement was crushed, and

the stones of the keep were scorched black. Hopefully, the walls were thick, and the timbers inside hadn't
been caught by the dragon's fire. "At least it still
stands," he pointed out. That was always a good sign.

Daniel let out a deep sigh and nodded. "For
now."

That was the truth if Patrick had ever heard it.
They were going to need to call on the king's masons
to check the stability of the structure. It would not
do to move into a castle that could fall on your head
at any moment.

Patrick clenched his jaw as they rode unchal-
lenged through the open gates. The place looked de-
serted. That was a bad sign. The lord of the castle may
be dead, but surly there should have been someone
tending the keep. Looking over the bailey, he understood why there was no one here.

"Now that *is* a mess." Patrick sighed. Stone from
the wall littered the grounds, and all the outbuildings
were in cinders. Several charred bodies lay scattered
around. At least they had died quickly. "Spread out
and look for survivors," he called to the men riding
in behind him. "Defend if you must, but remember,
we are here to help, not conquer. Bring anyone you
find to the main hall."

An agreeing murmur sounded from the men as
they dismounted to search.

Patrick slid from his horse and handed the reins to one of his men. "Let's get this over with." He and Daniel loosened their swords as they mounted the steps to the main keep. The door was shut but swung open when they pushed on it.

"Hello?" Patrick called into the darkness inside. The only answer was the flutter of feathers as his voice echoed eerily around the empty chamber. Everything looked to be intact, but the main hearth was cold—something rarely seen in a castle, even in the summer months.

"I don't think anyone's home." Daniel pushed the second door wide to let the afternoon light in. It cut through some of the darkness but left a lot of the room in shadow.

"Let's see what we can find," Patrick said. They were going to need torches to explore the darkness. Fishing for the flint in his pouch, he struck it on the steel of the fire cauldron by the door. The sparks should have caught on oiled tinder, but they died in cold ash. So much for the easy way.

Daniel chuckled as he scraped some of the dried thresh from the floor and tossed it into the metal bowl. "Try it now."

Patrick shook his head and struck the flint, again dropping sparks. This time, fire caught in the kindling. Looking around, the two men found wood and fed the flames until they glowed brightly.

"Stay where you are."

The men froze at the sound of a young voice. Slowly, they turned to face a boy, maybe eight or ten, holding a sword that was much too large for him.

"Good day." Patrick raised his hand showing he meant no threat. "I've come to speak with the lord of the castle."

"He's dead," the boy barked. "Now go away."

"Then who is the master here?"

The boy brandished his sword in threat. "I am. Now leave."

Patrick shot Daniel an intrigued look.

The corners of the other man's mouth turned up slightly in amusement.

"Who's there, Christian?" The voice of a woman sounded from the doorway behind the lad. A light was steadily growing, pushing back the gloom.

"No one, Nana. Go back to the kitchen," the boy called over his shoulder.

"Of course there is someone." A woman stepped through the opening. "I may be old, but I can still hear." The woman was old, but she was not yet twisted with age. Her white hair glittered brightly in the light from her candle. She lifted it high, so the light would shine across the great hall.

"Just bandits." The boy raised his sword again. Its

weight was too great, and the tip kept sinking to the floor.

A quick cuff to the side of the boy's head made his sword *thunk* to the ground. "Christian Zyler! Your mother raised you better than this," she scolded as the boy raised a hand to the aching side of his head. "How dare you call these fine young men bandits."

Patrick raised an amused eyebrow. Standing taller than most of their men, with a shock of copper red hair, he supposed he must be striking to look at. He glanced over at Daniel, with his brown hair and body toned from hours of hard work. Yes, they did make a fine pair, although they were well worn from days of travel.

"Please forgive my grandson." The woman turned her attention back to the two men. "We've had nothing but problems since the dragon came."

"Understandable." Patrick stepped towards them with his hands held wide.

The boy raised his sword, making the old woman cuff him again.

It was hard to keep the amusement off his face, but Patrick managed the feat. It wouldn't do to provoke the lad by laughing. "My name is Patrick Mylan. I've been sent by the king to see about this dragon problem."

The old woman nodded. "Oh, praise the Lord."

She sighed and lowered her candle. "I thought we were doomed to die by that beast."

Lowering his hands, he came closer to the woman. "Where is everyone?" Patrick looked around the great hall as if people would pop out of the shadows.

"Dead or gone." The woman turned back towards the opening in the wall. "Christian and I are all that are left."

Patrick shot Daniel a concerned look and followed the woman and her grandson into the hallway. "What happened?"

The sigh the woman let out was depressing. She led the way to the kitchen, where a fire burned brightly in the hearth and the smell of cooking food made Patrick's stomach grumble. "After the dragon started ravaging the outer farms, the town's men called on Lord Dunham to protect them. He thought he could handle it."

She settled her candle into a sconce on the wall and went to a chair near the fire. "He called up the men of the village, supplied them with weapons, and was teaching them to fight when the dragon arrived. The first attack went well. They drove the creature off, but it was soon back. It crushed the wall and killed the lord and half of the men before leaving." Horror passed behind the woman's eyes as she spoke.

Her grandson settled on the floor next to her,

trying to give her some comfort.

She smiled down at the boy and rubbed his golden curls. "In a fit of rage and grief, the lord's son took what men remained to hunt the creature in the hills. Only the dragon returned to scorch the castle. The lady of the castle and several of the hands died in the fires that night. Then, the dragon snatched up one of the scullery maids and left."

"But where are the rest of the servants?" Patrick looked around. Two pallets were laid out along the walls of the kitchen. The old woman and lad must be living in this room, terrified to leave.

"Gone." The woman sighed. "Every third day, the dragon returned to ravage the castle. He only left when a maiden was sent out to appease his wrath." Tears hung in her eyes. "After the third maiden was taken, most of the staff packed up what they could carry and left. When the dragon came back again, it killed the few that remained and turned its attention to the town, only stopping when it claimed another maiden."

"How did you and the young man escape?" Daniel inquired.

Shame etched the old woman's face. "We were out picking herbs for my hands." She held out her gnarled hands. "They hurt when it rains."

Daniel nodded.

"When we came back, the castle was empty and the dragon had already laid waste to the town. We had nowhere else to go."

The way she said those words made Patrick's heart ache.

"Fear not." Patrick pressed a fist over his heart and bowed to her. "We have come and will end this dragon."

The look the old woman gave him was skeptical. "You have two days until the dragon returns for his next maiden."

The woman's words hung heavily in Patrick's heart. "Then we will get on it straight away." He turned to Daniel. "Call the men together and ask for volunteers. Pick ten and place them at guard on the walls. I don't want to be caught unaware if this dragon returns early."

Daniel nodded. "And the rest?"

"Divide them up. Send half to clean out the castle and relight the fires and the rest to clear the bailey."

Daniel left to carry out Patrick's instructions.

Patrick turned back to the old woman. "Forgive me, My Lady. I do not wish to invade, but I must claim this castle in the name of the king. I assure you that you and your grandson are safe and welcome to stay, but I need a place to house my men."

"As you wish, My Lord." The old woman bowed

her head to Patrick. "No one will protest your claim as long as you slay the dragon."

"And that is what I intend to do." Patrick turned to head back out to his men. There was much work to be done before the dragon returned, and it would all have to be done in human form.

"Daniel!" Patrick yelled as he reached the opening to the main hall.

Daniel stopped in the doorway to wait.

"I want two men to scout—Douglas and Mathew. Their lesser forms are the smallest. Send them to the tower in the back to shift and fly out. I want a full report on the area around the town. I want to know where this dragon is."

Daniel nodded again.

"But remind them to stay out of sight. This area is already frantic about one dragon. The last thing we need is them worried about more."

"A wise decision," Daniel agreed. "And where will you be?"

"I will be heading to the town to secure supplies." Patrick looked in the direction of the village. "We are going to need tithing to support this place."

Shock rooted Daniel to the floor. "We haven't even settled in yet."

"Yes, and the sooner the village understands we're here to protect them, the sooner we'll get the supplies we need." Patrick started down the steps towards his horse. "Oh," he paused and turned back to Daniel, "and tell the men they will have to move the rubble by hand. There are humans here, and I want no dragons seen." The men were not going to like that, but it was to be expected.

The village was nearly as bad as Dunham Castle. More than half of the small, stone-and-thatch buildings were damaged or burned. People watched Patrick as he rode into the main square—mostly women and children. He almost felt bad about asking the town to support his troops, but they were there to help these people.

"My name is Patrick Mylan." His voice echoed around the village square. "I wish to speak with the head of the village."

A murmur circled the townspeople.

"He's dead."

Patrick turned in his saddle to face the young woman answering him. She was beautiful. Standing slightly taller than the other girls, her long, dark hair flowed around her heart-shaped face.

Hitching her chin up in defiance, she went on. "He died when Lord Dunham provoked the dragon."

"So who now speaks for the town?" Patrick smiled at her. He liked a girl with spunk.

The woman opened her mouth to answer but was cut off before she could.

"I do."

Patrick turned towards the voice calling from the other side of the square.

An elderly man stepped from the crowd.

"And your name, my good man?" Patrick asked.

"Eustace," he answered.

Great—a man of many words. Patrick drew in a calming breath before going on. It was going to take every ounce of diplomacy his mother had taught him to make these people agree to his request. "I am Patrick Mylan," he restated. "I have been sent by the king to see to your dragon."

This sent another murmur through the gathering crowd.

"I claim Dunham Castle as my payment."

Silence flowed across the crowd.

Patrick went on. "She is in need of much repair. I will require a tithing from the town."

A roar of objection went up.

After a moment, the crowd quieted enough for Patrick to continue. "In return for your support, I will rid you of your dragon and offer you the protection of a lord."

Outrage swept through the villagers.

"How do you expect us to pay a tithing? The dragon has razed all of our crops and killed most of our men." The sweet voice of the woman cut through the din.

Patrick turned back to her. "I understand that times are hard, and I have coin enough to pay for the supplies I need for now. The tithing I ask is for repairs to the castle *after* I've vanquished the dragon." He looked around at the now-silent faces. "It's no more than any lord would ask of his people."

"We are *not* your people," the woman snapped at him.

Oh yes, she was feisty, but so was he. Patrick smiled back at her. "Then I will leave you to your dragon, fair maiden." Pulling on the reins of his horse, he turned back towards the castle.

"Wait." Eustace held up his hand to stop Patrick from leaving. "Can you really slay this dragon?"

"My men and I are well versed in the ways of dragons." Patrick bowed his head. "We can stop this beast."

"And what happens when you fail?" the feisty woman yelled at his back.

Patrick turned in his saddle to look back at her. "Then you will be left with a fat dragon and be free of the tithing," he sassed before turning his attention back to Eustace. "My men and I will be down in two days' time, ready to defend you from this dragon. Please think upon my offer."

He glanced back over his shoulder at the feisty woman. "In the meantime, you may want to think about which maiden the dragon would like to eat next." Indignation turned the woman's face red as he turned his horse back towards the castle and kicked it into a run.

Rage clenched Kathryn's throat as she watched that pompous ass ride away. Patrick Mylan. Of all the self-centered, arrogant men she had ever met, he took the cake. How *dare* he come down here and demand a tithing to fix up that blasted castle! The thing had been empty yesterday! He was just as bad as that fatheaded Dunham, with all his taxes. And the one time they had asked him for help, he riled up the dragon and got the men of the village killed.

Kathryn stewed as she crossed the village square to where Eustace stood contemplating the man riding out of sight. "You cannot be thinking about agreeing to this," she said, starting in on the elder.

Eustace turned considering eyes to her. "And what would you have me do?" he asked. "If we just let things go, the dragon will kill us all. Besides, we did ask the king to send help. Did you expect it to come without a price?"

Kathryn stared at him silently, unable to answer his question.

"You are not the only one that's lost family to this dragon," Eustace pointed out. "I've lost two sons already. I don't want to lose my granddaughter as well."

Kathryn let out a deep sigh. "But, we can't let him rile up this dragon more," she pleaded. "It might destroy the whole town." This was a touchy subject for them all. So many of the girls were left without a protector. They didn't need someone else coming in to ruffle the dragon's scales again. It might not stop at taking just one girl at a time.

"And which maiden do you suggest we send next?" Eustace asked, his temper starting to rise. "Mary? She's only twelve. Constance? Her mother is old and weak. How about you?"

Kathryn clenched her jaw, holding back her anger. The old man had a point.

"No." Eustace slashed his hand through the air, killing her refusal of Patrick's offer. "I will bring this up with the other elders." He turned to go.

"But, he's a fool," Kathryn exclaimed as she followed him. "No man could stand against such a creature."

"Enough, Kathryn," Eustace chided her. "I will speak with the others on this."

Dropping back, Kathryn let the old man go. There was no reason to argue with him once he got an idea in his head. She looked up at the castle to where Patrick had ridden. "You will be the death of us all."

Who knew death could come in such a handsome package?

Patrick pushed his way into the great hall. The place looked a hell of a lot better now. A fire crackled warmly in the hearth, and debris had been cleared from the floor. Several of the men had sat down to plates of dried meat and cheese—part of the rations they had brought with them.

"So how did it go?" Daniel asked.

"They think I'm a fool." Patrick dropped himself onto a bench near the fire.

Daniel raised an eyebrow and pushed a trencher of food towards his friend.

Patrick leaned on the table and picked out a piece of cheese. "Of course, they would think any man that would take on a dragon a fool." Popping the cheese in his mouth, he laid his head and shoulder on the table.

"Did they agree to the tithing?" Daniel asked.

Laughing, Patrick shook his head. "No." He picked up a chunk of dried meat and looked at it. "But, I also told them we would be down to watch the dragon eat the next maiden should they not change their minds." Sticking the end of the meat in his mouth, he gnawed on it.

"Patrick!" Daniel scolded. "The prince will be furious if we let this dragon eat any more maidens."

"I know that." Patrick chomped away on his tid-bit as he talked. "I will do everything in my power to see this dragon is stopped before he can take another life, but *they* don't know that."

Daniel cocked an inquisitive eyebrow at him.

"I didn't go down to the village expecting them to agree to the tithing. No man would willingly give up a tenth of his goods. I went down to threaten them with the dragon." Patrick tapped his finger on the table, emphasizing his words. "Either *pay* the tith-ing, or we *let* the dragon eat you. When you put it that way, the village will be happy to support us once we've stopped the dragon."

The man's audacity left Daniel staring at him speechlessly. After a moment, he regained his wit and laughed. "You, my friend, are a crafty man."

Patrick just shrugged.

"So in two days' time, we go to kill a dragon."

"No." Patrick shook his head and poked at the food, looking for another enticing morsel. "In two days, we go in human form to turn the dragon from the village."

"In human form?" Daniel asked, shocked. "Now you *are* being a fool. The task you suggest is impossible, even with two squads of men."

"Two score plus you and I—all Elites in Eternity. We've trained for this. If we can't turn one dragon back in human form, then we don't deserve the name of Elite," Patrick pointed out. "Anyway, I don't intend for us to kill the beast initially."

Daniel raised an eyebrow. "What are you playing at?"

"I intend a show." Patrick pushed the trencher away. He was hungry, but the food was too dry for his taste. A glass of something was needed to help get it down. "Something to prove to the village that we can protect them."

A slow nod moved Daniel. Finally, the man was starting to see Patrick's point.

"Have Douglas and Mathew returned yet?"

"Not yet."

"I need a full report when they do." Patrick pushed himself into a more respectable position. "I want to know where his lair is. Once we've played for the public, we'll go deal with this dragon properly."

33

This brought a smile to Daniel's face. "I knew there was a reason Kyle sent you," he laughed. "I would have just killed it outright and been done."

Patrick stood up from the table. "And you would have spent the next year subduing the village to get what you needed."

Daniel laughed again. "Better a hero than a tyrant."

"Exactly. Now, if you'll excuse me, I'm going to see if I can find something to help with this." Patrick waved at the dry food before leaving for the kitchen. This place had to have a wine cellar somewhere.

Chapter Three

Two long lines marched from Dunham Castle to the village. Patrick looked over the men, approving of their preparations. Each wore a suit of light, leather armor and carried a huge metal shield. Half carried long swords, and the rest had spears. With a light mist falling from the sky, it was a perfect day to tangle with a dragon.

Daniel hefted up his shield and followed his men. "Let's hope your ploy works." There were only fifteen fighters ready to do battle. The rest were already spread throughout the countryside, waiting.

"I hope so, too," Patrick admitted. This plan would have been better if Douglas and Mathew had been able to locate the dragon's lair, but now they had to track it back to its home before they could deal with it.

"If we get the opportunity to kill him, I think we should take it," Daniel pointed out.

"Most definitely," Patrick agreed, "but I don't

think he'll give us one."

"You never know." Daniel shrugged. "If he's gone in his head, he might leave himself open."

"Point, but I don't want anyone getting hurt during this." Patrick looked at the men. "I don't want heroes taking stupid risks."

"As if this whole thing isn't a stupid risk," Daniel scoffed, earning a glare from Patrick. "I understand why it's needed, but it's still dangerous."

"And we've talked about this," Patrick agreed. "If he turns on us, we'll shift and take him on, but I'd rather not have that in front of the villagers. You know how the king feels about exposing ourselves to humans."

Daniel nodded.

"Let's just stick to the plan, and we'll be okay."

The hike from the castle to the town was relatively short. The men stopped just outside of the village and let Patrick and Daniel lead the way in.

"Good morrow, Eustace," Patrick greeted the familiar face in the crowd. He nodded to the woman he had swapped wits with on his previous visit. "Fair maiden."

She stood proudly next to the village elder, shooting a look of pure hatred at Patrick.

Patrick gave his attention back to Eustace. "Have you considered my offer," his eyes shifted to the woman in white next to him, "or have you chosen your maiden?"

Rage colored her face.

Eustace gripped her forearm to silence her before she spewed the venomous words Patrick could see flash in her lovely, blue eyes. "We are considering your offer," the town elder answered, "but we have chosen a maiden."

The color washed out of the girl's face as she clenched her jaw.

"If you can protect her and the village, then we will agree to your terms."

"As you wish." Patrick bowed, earning him an eye roll from the girl. "Please tell me everything you can about the dragon and how he's been collecting these maidens."

Kathryn stood back as she listened to Eustace talk with the new lord. She glared at him, hoping the dragon would eat him when it showed up.

"Good morrow, fair maiden."

A dark-haired man approached her. He wasn't quite as tall as Patrick, but he was ruggedly handsome. His dark eyes shimmered as she greeted him. "Good morrow, My Lord."

Laughter bubbled out of him. "He," the man nodded to Patrick, "will be your new lord. I am but his humble servant." Picking up her hand, the man bent over and kissed its back. "I am Daniel."

A blush rose in Kathryn's cheeks. She was not used to such treatment from men. "Kathryn," she said as she dropped him a curtsey.

"So, are you the maiden we are here to protect?" Daniel asked. His eyes dropped, taking in the flowing white gown she wore.

Unused to the attentions of such a handsome man, she nodded shyly.

He gave her a reassuring smile. "Would you like to meet your defenders?"

Kathryn nodded, still at a loss for words. This man was nothing like the arrogant ass who had come down demanding a tithing.

Daniel tucked her hand around his arm to escort her down the lines of men.

Her eyes wandered them curiously. These men looked ill prepared for the battle to come. Although they did have weapons and large shields, they lacked the plate armor knights wore. Their light leathers dripped with water from the drizzle that had just stopped. Patrick must have had them standing out in the rain for hours before marching them down here. Was he abusing these men before sending them to their deaths? *What a tyrant!* Kathryn wrinkled her nose in disgust as they came back around to stand next to the man in question.

"The dragon will come from the south." Patrick pointed to the open field just past the edge of the village. "We'll line up one hundred paces from the village. That should be far enough away to keep the flames from the thatch roofs."

"Better make it a hundred and fifty; we don't know how hot he is," Daniel suggested.

Nodding his agreement, Patrick finally turned his attention to the young woman holding Daniel's arm.

"May I introduce you to the fair maiden you're here to protect?" Daniel released Kathryn's hand and pushed her forward a step. "This is Kathryn."

A smile slipped into Patrick's eyes, and he took up her hand and kissed it.

She shivered with the urge to snatch her hand away and wipe it on her gown.

"It's a pleasure to finally meet you, fair maiden." Patrick turned her and wrapped her hand around his arm.

Kathryn's eyes widened in shock; he was as wet as his men.

He stepped onto the curved edge of an oversize shield, popping it up so he could grab the handle without bending over. It was an action she could tell he had done before. Maybe he practiced it to look suave.

"Fear not," he said, maneuvering the shield into place as he talked, "we will turn your dragon this day." Pulling her along, he led the way to the edge of the field, leaving Daniel to bark orders at the assembled men.

He wasn't even going to order his own men around! Kathryn glared at him. There was no way this man would make a decent lord, even if he survived the dragon.

The dragon was huge! It stood ten feet tall at the shoulder, and its mouth was large enough to fit a full-sized man. His scales were black as obsidian, and a boned frill protected the back of his head. A beautiful specimen. It was such a shame that they were going to have to kill him.

"You're going to take on *that* with a few swords and shields?" Kathryn sassed.

Patrick had to hand it to her. Even knowing she was going to die if he failed, she still had spunk. "Of course not, my fair maiden." He smiled at her. "I'm going to use words."

The look she shot him clearly said he was insane.

He patted her hand reassuringly as they waited for the dragon to approach. They stood at the center of a wall of men ready to defend the town.

The dragon stopped and considered them for a moment. His eyes fell on Kathryn before looking at the rest of the men.

Giving her one more reassuring pat, Patrick released her. Turning to where he had dropped his shield while the men formed ranks, he stomped on the edge of the disk again. The hard metal popped up, and he caught it with the same flare as before. "Wait here while I reason with him." He turned his attention to Daniel. "Keep her safe."

Daniel took up a protective position next to her.

"Good morrow!" Patrick called out as he walked into the field with the dragon.

The dragon cocked his head curiously.

"I am Patrick Mylan of Eternity. By order of the king, I demand that you end your harassment of this village. If you surrender now and come along peacefully, your trial will be just and your sentence lenient. If you refuse, you will force us to take swift action to defend these people."

The dragon blinked a few times as he drew in a deep breath.

Seeing the attack coming, Patrick dropped down

41

and raised his shield. A great blast of fire washed over the hardened steel, heating the metal. Grabbing the pouch at his side, he tucked it up so the flames licking around the edges of his shield wouldn't set it alight. As soon as the onslaught stopped, Patrick rose to face his attacker.

The dragon looked at him. The cock of its great head showed its confusion.

Steam rose from the man's soaked leathers, but Patrick was mostly unharmed. "It would do you good to use your nose before you attacked," he taunted. "I know a thing or two about dragons."

The dragon twisted his head the other way before opening his mouth to try to roast the lord again.

Taking aim, Patrick threw the pouch from his side into the dragon's open mouth before dropping back down behind his shield again. A second blast of fire hit him just before the pouch exploded in the dragon's mouth. The shock knocked Patrick back to the ground, and the creature's flames were cut off as it coughed. Black smoke boiled out of its mouth. It shook its head violently before staggering off-balance. A shudder ran down the creature's body before it took wing and retreated.

Dropping the red-hot shield, Patrick tried to stagger up and away from the charred grass. He stumbled and fell backwards onto his butt as Daniel and Kathryn ran to check on him.

The men held their line in case the dragon changed its mind.

"What the hell did you put in that?" Daniel asked as he bent to his friend.

Patrick looked at him, dazed. "*What?*" he yelled, putting his finger into his ear and rubbing it furiously. His entire head rang from the explosion.

"*What did you put in that?*" Daniel yelled, articulating his words more carefully.

Leaning back onto the heels of his hands, Patrick looked up at his friend. "Just the normal stuff." He wasn't quite yelling now, but his voice was a lot louder than it normally was. "Pine pitch, wood dust, saltpeter, sage, clove, sulfur… oh, and I added some charcoal." The questioning look Daniel gave him made Patrick shrug. "I thought it would make it smoke more. I wasn't expecting it to pop like that."

Daniel reached his hand down to help Patrick up. "Where did you get that idea?"

The downed man looked at it for a moment before grasping it. "The king's last birthday," he explained as Daniel raised him to his feet. His friend took most of his weight as Patrick tried to find his balance. "I stole one of the sky fires."

Daniel just chuckled.

Kathryn gasped. "Your arm."

The note of dismay in her voice drew Patrick's attention before he dropped his gaze to the hand he'd been holding the shield with. The skin on his wrist and forearm was blistered from the heat. "That's nothing." Patrick held on to Daniel as he kicked at his shield and flipped the thing over with the toe of his boot. The center of the large disk was blackened and warped.

Kathryn bent over it, shocked.

Daniel raised an appreciative eyebrow. "His fire was nearly as hot as yours."

Patrick nodded. "I will endeavor to get it hotter next time." That second blast of flame had almost been too much for the metal. As it was, the leather padding on the back was going to need to be replaced. Even after being soaked in water, the dragon had cooked that protection clean off.

"What kind of metal stands up to dragon fire?" Kathryn asked, holding her hand out towards the hot surface.

Patrick looked down at the ruined shield. The telltale marks of its forging ran across the surface like water, making it easy to recognize, but this type of metal wasn't seen very often in this area.

"Damascus steel, forged in dragon's fire," Patrick answered. Feeling a little more stable on his feet, he released Daniel to stand on his own.

44

Kathryn glared up at him. "You use dragons to forge your shields?" The accusation was heavy in her voice.

Patrick shrugged. "Not all dragons are bad." He had been forging his own shields for a while now. When he'd first entered training, he had relied on others to craft his weapons, and one had failed during a particularly nasty session. Those burns made the one on his arm look like a scratch. Thankfully, he had healed well.

"What would have happened if he had tried to eat you instead?" Kathryn asked, standing away from the cooling metal.

A smile curled the edge of Patrick's lips. He flipped the shield back over with his foot. "He would have had a really bad day. The edge is sharp as a sword." Stepping on the edge of the bowl, he tried gathering it up again, but the metal had warped so it didn't come up as far as it had before. Patrick lunged for it, trying to catch it, but he hadn't fully recovered from the explosion. The quick motion made him stumble.

Kathryn grabbed him before he could fall onto the hot shield.

"Sorry." Leaning into her shoulder, he swallowed hard. His head had started spinning, and it wasn't doing his stomach any good.

45

Daniel chuckled at him. "If you can help him back to his men, I'll get his shield." Stepping on the edge of the shield, he popped it up and grabbed the handle without touching the hot metal.

Kathryn watched in amazement. Apparently, that skill wasn't just to look good. She held Patrick up as Daniel took the shield away. The new lord looked a little green. "Come on." She shifted to his side and pulled his arm over her shoulder.

He leaned on her and stumbled back towards the town. "Thanks."

Wrapping her arm around his back, she found that his leather armor was now dry. She pondered this as they walked. Had he not been wet, that flame might very well have cooked him. "You had your men soak their leathers before coming down this morning."

Patrick gave her a considering look before answering. "Wet leather is the last line of defense when dealing with a dragon." He sighed before going on. "Although, facing off with a dragon with anything can be folly if his fire is hot enough."

Kathryn shook her head. "Yet you went out with just a shield."

Patrick shrugged. "I had my smoke packs."

"Those were impressive, but they didn't kill it."

"I would rather not kill him if I didn't have to."

This statement made Kathryn stop, jarring Patrick to a halt. "*What?*" she snapped indignantly. After the dragon had killed so many, the lord didn't want to destroy the thing? Kathryn nearly dropped the man where they stood.

Patrick groaned in pain and raised his hand up to his head. "I wanted to give him the chance to surrender," he explained. "Rouge dragons are hard to take down."

Kathryn stared at him openmouthed. She couldn't believe her ears. He spoke as if he had fought with dragons before.

Pulling on her, Patrick tried to get her moving again.

Taking him in her arms again, she helped him to his men. He wasn't looking very good at all. "Can you kill this thing?" she asked.

"Yes." Patrick sounded confident. "We will stop this dragon."

Kathryn mentally tacked the words 'or die trying' on the end for him.

The line of men now stood loose as they watched her approach with their leader.

"Douglas. Mathew." Patrick tried to yell, but it

ended on more of a whimper.

Two men stepped forward.

His voice was quieter as he went on. "Go back to the castle and change. Head out to the scouts and call any that aren't chasing the dragon home. It went south. Send a few to search that way in case any of our men ran into trouble. And stay out of sight. Remember, we are scouting, not confronting."

The two men clasped their fists to their chests and bowed before taking off towards the castle.

Patrick stood up away from Kathryn, but he still wobbled on his feet and was a little pale. Kathryn was reluctant to let the poor man go. He was still looking mighty shaken.

"Daniel." Patrick looked around for his friend.

Kathryn looked around and found the man coming towards them. He had just finished sending Patrick's damaged shield off with a group of men heading towards the castle.

"I've picked five to remain in the village in case the dragon comes back," Daniel informed them.

Patrick gave him a shallow nod. "If he feels anything like I do, I don't think he'll be back today."

Both Daniel and Kathryn reached out to grab Patrick as he wobbled on his feet again.

"Shouldn't they change out of their wet leathers?" Kathryn asked, concerned for the men. They would catch a terrible chill if they remained soaking wet.

Patrick tried to shake his head, but stopped. The color in his face went a little green, and he swallowed hard before he spoke. "It's best if they remain ready in case it does."

Daniel pulled Patrick's arm over his shoulder, taking his weight. "I think we should get you back so you can rest." He turned slightly to look at Kathryn. "We have turned your dragon and will continue to hunt it."

Kathryn gave him a slow, acknowledging nod.

"You are safe now, My Lady." With that, Daniel turned and half-dragged Patrick's stumbling form back to the castle.

"He did it," Eustace said as he stepped up next to Kathryn and watched the men stagger away.

"Yes," she answered him, deep in thought. *He did turn the dragon today, but how was he going to defeat it?*

"I think this new lord may be worth the tithing he's asked." Eustace patted her on the arm and turned to go report to the other elders.

She let out a long breath before heading to her own home. Maybe her initial impression of him was wrong. Maybe he was a kind and caring man. He had seemed genuinely worried about his men. Then again, he could just be rattled by that explosion. He had been rather close to it.

Kathryn nodded her head, accepting that as the answer. No caring man would ride into a town and demand one tenth of the village's earnings. She clenched her jaw, setting her heart and mind against him. He was a tyrant, there to bend them to his will, not a handsome man who had just risked his life to protect her. The first she could handle; the second might endanger her heart.

"Are you sure you should head out in your condition?" Daniel asked, trying to change Patrick's mind. "I could take the report to the prince."

Pushing the bedding back, Patrick got up. He knew he shouldn't travel after his encounter with the dragon, but he had a duty to see to. "I don't need to shirk my responsibilities onto you." His headache was much better now that he'd rested. As he prepared to leave, Patrick didn't bother with his clothing draped over the foot of the bed. Christian and his grandmother would be in the kitchen, and the rest of the men understood. "I promised the prince an update when we confronted the dragon, and I will take it to him."

"I don't think he meant for you to fly if you were

injured."

Patrick looked down at his left arm. The skin was blistered from his fingers clear up to his elbow on the outer edge, and the rest of his arm was red.

"I didn't realize you were hurt that badly. You're lucky you didn't shift."

An ironic laugh slipped out of Patrick. "His fire was hotter than I expected, and that smoke pack had quite a punch." He looked up at his friend. "But there was nothing to worry about. I don't usually shift when injured." He paused as the events of the day passed through his mind. "You did make sure to tell everyone to keep those things away from heat?"

"After watching yours go up, I think they got the idea." The corner of Daniel's mouth turned up. "I've heard a few of the men writing limericks about it already."

Patrick hung his head. "Oh dear." For as long as he had been training, the short rhymes had been the men's way of immortalizing heroic acts of idiocy. It had been a point of pride that he could claim he'd managed to avoid the honor so far. "And what are they saying?" he asked, not really wanting to know.

"It's not as bad as you think." Daniel cleared his throat and recited the rhyme. "When faced with a dragon of black, Patrick took a gift from his sack. When faced with the flame, he calmly took aim, and

51

thwarted the critter's attack."

"That's not bad at all." His first limerick, and it told of something good he'd done.

"That's the best of the ones I heard." Daniel grinned. "There were a few others that were more amusing, but they lacked the right cadence to be any good. Would you like me to recite them?"

Patrick shook his head. "No, I think that one is more than enough." He looked towards the window. The light of day was waning. "Dusk is drawing near. I should get ready to head out."

"Will you be able to find your way in the dark?"

Waving the older man's worries away, Patrick reassured him. "I've made my way to the prince many times in the dark. I'll make it just fine. It's finding my way back here that might be the issue." Patrick had gotten very used to night flights since the king had banned dragons from flying in the day around humans. It was easier to keep their presence secret if there weren't dragon sightings all the time.

Daniel nodded.

"Once I've gone, put a caldron up on the tallest tower. That should help."

Daniel glanced towards the window at the fading light. "Here's a thought. Why don't you go ahead and shift into your lesser form and circle the castle a few times so you can recognize it? That way, you'll be less likely to miss it on your way back."

"Excellent idea." Patrick closed his eyes and relaxed. Magic tingled over his skin as red scales shimmered down his side. He stretched his wings before folding them back. Patrick's lesser form was slightly larger than his human form.

Daniel eyed him. "Geez, you're big."

A grumbling reply met him. Patrick disliked that about his lesser form. Most of the other dragons were small in their lesser forms. They ranged from the size of house cats to large dogs. It made it easier to slip out in scales and relax, but Patrick couldn't get out as often. The real kicker was, his grand form was only slightly larger. He was too big to do anything stealthy, yet too small to do any heavy work.

Daniel held the door open for him. "You'd better go out the front. I don't think you'll fit through the trap door to the tower."

Great… another disadvantage to his size. Patrick huffed and headed out. He paused in the hall long enough to make sure no one was around before slinking along the corridor. His passing in the great hall turned a few heads, but they simply nodded at him.

"My Lord."

The voice stopped Patrick before he could reach the main door. He turned around as Douglas jogged up to him.

53

"I'm glad I caught you before you left."

Curling his tail around his feet, Patrick sat up. "Did you find him?" he chirped in dragon.

Douglas shook his head. "No, My Lord. We followed it south, but lost it in the forest." The man looked downcast and weary. "He must have shifted to human."

Patrick nodded. "At least we know where to start our search tomorrow." He turned his gaze to Daniel. "We should probably keep men in the village until he's caught." Pausing, he thought for a moment. Being in dragon form brought him closer to his instincts, and something was nagging at them. He just couldn't place what it was. "If he comes back, use the smoke packs to drive him off, and send the scouts to follow. I want to understand this dragon before we have to kill it."

"We should take the opportunity to kill it if we can," Daniel objected.

"True," Patrick agreed, "but something doesn't sit right in here." The fringy end of his tail came up and patted him in the chest. "I don't know how to explain it, but I get the feeling there's more going on."

Daniel just cocked his head and shrugged.

Patrick turned his attention back to Douglas. "Anyway, thank you for the update. I must be off." Uncurling, he headed for the door. He still had a long night ahead of him if he planned to be home before dawn.

Mmmm. Patrick sighed as he slipped into the cool water of the lake. It had taken most of the night to get to the prince and give his report. Kyle had insisted on having someone look at his wound before letting him leave again. After a nice meal and some rest, the prince had finally let Patrick making the flight back. With dawn quickly approaching, he should have just gone straight back to the castle, but the burn on his front leg stung, and the water from the lake looked so cool.

Tucking his wings in, Patrick dove deeper into the lake. It had been some time since he had last been out in scales, and even longer since his last swim. Lashing his tail back and forth, he zipped through the water. He loved the way the water swished over his hide. He could do this all day.

A flash of silver to his left set off his hunting instincts, and he snapped at the fish. He missed, and the thing flashed away into the murky waters of the lake. Patrick let it go; he wasn't hungry at the moment, although the thought of fresh fish for dinner did sound like a wonderful idea. For a moment, he considered just staying there for a while. Cool water to soothe his hurt, sunlight to warm his scales, and plenty of fish to eat. He could see why some dragons went feral. Letting out a long breath, he burst from the surface and flapped hard, shedding water as he gained height. The sun was almost up, and he needed to get back before the village woke up.

Clothing spilt across the ground from the basket Kathryn had dropped. The two other girls who had come to do their washing also stood in silence as horror stole over them. A red dragon had just burst from the lake and taken flight. There was another dragon in the area!

Kathryn turned around and grabbed her companions, pushing them towards the village. It only took the shocked girls a second to abandon their loads and retreat as fast as they could. Thankfully, they hadn't screamed when the creature broke the water's surface. Had they drawn its attention, they might not have made it out alive.

Chapter Four

"PATRICK." DANIEL'S VOICE ECHOED THROUGH THE darkened room.

A growl rumbled back in response.

"Wake up, Patrick."

Patrick cracked his eye and glared at the man disturbing him. "What?" he grumbled. Last night had been taxing, and he hadn't been sleeping for very long.

"The villagers have arrived with your tithing." There was a smile in the man's voice.

What the hell could make him that cheery this early in the morning? "Fine," Patrick muttered as he rolled over. "Put it away, and I'll check it out later." He snuggled back down into his blankets.

"Oh, no." Daniel had the nerve to come in and rip the covers off. "You need to see this."

Sitting up, Patrick glared at him. "I've had no sleep, and I'm hurt. Can't it wait until later?"

"No. Now, come on." Daniel threw Patrick's

clothing at him.

Growling, Patrick pulled them on and followed his friend down to the main hall. Running his hand through his sleep-mussed hair, Patrick's brain couldn't comprehend what he was seeing.

Ten woman, ranging from about twelve to around twenty, stood in the main hall. Each held a basket of what looked to be linens. Several of the men stood around the edges of the room, staring at them. Patrick rubbed his eye with a knuckle as he walked through the girls towards the town elder standing near the door.

The girls curtsied as he passed.

"Good morrow, My Lord," Eustace greeted Patrick.

It was good to see the man was accepting him as his lord. "Good morrow," Patrick returned the greeting. "What's this?" He waved to the women standing around.

Eustace bowed to him. "I apologize for waking you up, My Lord. I've brought part of your tithing."

Patrick stood up as if someone had splashed him with water. The note in the old man's voice was grave. "And the ladies?" Surely, they could not be part of the tithing.

"These are the few maidens left in the village," Eustace explained. "I humbly request that you take them in."

Now that really sent Patrick's brain reeling. His brow furrowed in confusion.

The village elder went on. "A dragon was spotted today at the lake. Not the black dragon you drove off—a red dragon. Much smaller."

The color bled from Patrick's face. *Hell.* Someone had seen him take his morning swim.

"And Justin claims to have seen a baby dragon to the south. The thing was so small that he wasn't sure what it was at first. But where there are babies, there must be a momma."

Oh hell! If they were basing the size of dragons off the black dragon, both he and whatever scout was seen would look like juveniles. "The maidens are safe in the village," Patrick reassured them. "My men and I will protect you from the dragons." How was he supposed to tell them they *were* the dragons?

"Please," Eustace begged, "there is no one to defend these ladies should one attack."

Letting out a forlorn sigh, Patrick nodded. It was his only choice. Having offered these people his protection, he couldn't turn them away without dealing with the perceived danger. That was not a good way to get started as their lord. He turned to Daniel, standing with a gleam in his eye. At least the man kept the ear-to-ear grin from his face. "Clear the men from the castle and find rooms for the maidens," Patrick ordered. "If any of them want to leave the castle grounds, please make sure they have an escort."

The smile moved from his eyes to his mouth as Daniel nodded and left to carry out the orders.

Patrick turned back to the town elder. "Your ladies are safe. Daniel will sort them out." He closed his eyes as weariness over took him. "If you'll excuse me, I'm still recovering from yesterday's activities."

"Of course, My Lord." Eustace bowed as Patrick retreated to the safety of his chambers.

Maidens! What was he going to do with a castle full of *maidens*?

Kathryn looked at the back of the retreating man. He looked awful. He was as pale as sun-bleached linen, with dark bags under his eyes. His left arm was so badly wrapped that part of the burn was exposed. The clothes he'd hastily pulled on and his sleep-rumpled hair made him look like a child. She just wanted to pull him into her arms and soothe away his pains.

Shaking this thought away, she turned to the girls around her. As the oldest among them, she would have to take care of the rest.

"Now remember," Eustace's voice cut through

the whispers that had started, "you are guests here. These men will protect you, but please do your best to make their lives easier."

An affirmative murmur slid through the women.

"Kathryn," he turned his attention to her, "make sure everyone is taken care of." He looked around at the men standing uneasily along the walls of the room.

Kathryn caught the warning in his voice and nodded her head. She would make sure that the girls' virtues were defended if need be.

After a few minutes, Daniel came back into the room, followed by several men carrying armloads of personal items. "Ladies, if you'll come with me, I'll show you to your rooms."

Gathering up their baskets, the girls followed Daniel as he led the way deeper into the castle.

Daniel held his hand out, gesturing to a hallway. "Choose whichever chambers you like." Most of the doors were open, waiting for new occupants. "You may need to change out the linens," Daniel warned. "The men and I will bunk in the barracks should you need us."

"And Lord Mylan?" Kathryn couldn't help but ask. His condition rested heavily on her mind.

Daniel pointed to the one door that was shut. "He rests in the chambers at the end of the hall. If there is anything else, please let me know." At that, he left the women to get settled into their new accommodations.

"Well, *that* was pleasant," one girl said sarcastically.

Kathryn hefted up her basket and led the way down the hall. "What did you expect, Lillian? We came in here, unannounced, and ran these men out of their new home. I wouldn't expect them to be happy to have us."

The girls fell quiet as they followed her.

"Well, go ahead and pick your rooms," Kathryn called, choosing the room across from Patrick's. It was the room farthest down the hall. She tried to convince herself that her choice was due to the fact she was leading this group and had nothing to do with her desire to check on the injured man.

Kathryn's nose wrinkled as she took in the small room. The bedding was rumpled, and there was a strange musk in the air. Setting her basket on the small chest at the foot of the bed, she quickly opened the window for some fresh air. This had definitely been the room of some man. If the rest of the rooms were as bad as this, they had a lot of work to do. These men didn't know the first thing about cleaning.

Sighing, Kathryn pulled the linens off the bed and wadded them up. If they started now, they should be able to wash the sheets and have them dry by nightfall. Then they could start on the rest of the castle.

A knock on the door pulled Patrick from his sleep. Maybe if he ignored it, whoever was knocking would go away.

The knock sounded again.

What the hell did Daniel want now? "Come in," Patrick growled. *This had better be good.*

"Forgive me, My Lord," a sweet voice sounded as the door opened.

"Kathryn?" Patrick's mind raced, trying to reason out what she was doing there. He pushed himself up to look over at his visitor.

Kathryn came in carrying a tray. "Yes, My Lord." A wonderful smell hit him, making his stomach protest its empty state. "I've brought you dinner." She set the tray on a table next to the dying fire.

"Dinner?" Patrick glanced towards the window to see that the light of day was starting to die out. Had he really slept that long?

"Come eat before it gets cold." Kathryn shifted the bowl and spoon onto the table before turning to the fire. She fed a few logs onto the cooling embers, rousing the flames to light the room.

Entranced by her movement, Patrick stared as her. Backlit by firelight, she seemed more elegant than she had in the village. His breath caught as she turned back to face him. Her hair shimmered in the soft light, enhancing her already beautiful face. Even the slight furrow in her brow and purse of her lips as she looked on him with irritation did nothing to take away from her grace.

Coming over, she pulled his covers back. "Get up, My Lord."

Patrick was grateful he had just fallen back to bed in his clothing instead of stripping out of them like he normally did.

"Daniel asked me to come check on your wounds."

Ah, so Daniel had a hand in this. Patrick let out a deep sigh. It would have been nice if she had come to him out of her own desires. He shook that thought away and got up. "My wounds are really not that bad." Lifting his arm up, he held it out so she could see the bandage falling off the burn. He'd put some salve on and had hastily wrapped it before going to bed.

Kathryn pursed her lips again.

Oh, how he wanted to kiss that look off her face. He took a deep breath, drawing in her sweet scent. The smell of soap and flowers hung heavy on her skin.

An undertone of woman rounded the beautiful fragrance out. It made him want to bury his face in her middle and breathe her in.

She reached over and pulled his arm out to examine it, making his skin sizzle under her gentle fingers. "You really should take better care of this." The way she poked at the burned arm made his toes curl in ecstasy. Even her touch on the sensitive injury was exquisite. He would gladly submit to her just to feel her delicate hands run over his bare skin.

Catching his thoughts before they could push him to action, Patrick shook his head and pulled his arm out of her grasp. "It's fine." He stepped around her and started towards the table and the meal she had brought. It was dangerous for a dragon to get too casual with a human. Even a kiss, properly given, could drive the strictest of ladies to great depths of passion. Kathryn was a maiden he was sworn to protect. He shouldn't be having these thoughts about her, no matter how well her dress hugged her form.

Spinning around, she grabbed him by the shoulder, stopping him. "It's not! It could sour if not properly tended."

Patrick spun in her grasp and snaked his good arm around her. Pulling her firmly against him, he looked down into her eyes. The fact that they widened in surprise drove him on. "Do you worry for me, my fair maiden?" he asked softly, searching her face as she stiffened in his embrace. They fit together so perfectly. Her heartbeat and breathing quickened as he watched desire and fear crawl across her features. Her mouth worked a little before she could finally find words.

"Only as much as one cares for their protector." Sliding her hands up to his chest, she made him give her some space.

Squeezing her again, he crushed her arms between them and bent his face in close to hers. "I can think of other ways a maiden could thank her savior." He spoke softly, almost against her lips. Both the fear and desire in her eyes deepened at his suggestive tone. He let his breath trickle over her skin.

She swallowed hard. The tip of her tongue darted out, wetting her lips.

For a moment, Patrick thought she would lean in to take his mouth. That thought stoked the fire in his soul. It was all he could do to keep from closing that gap himself and tasting her sweetness.

A blush crawled up her skin as she felt the change in his body. She pushed away from him. "Forgive me, My Lord." Kathryn pulled from his arms and disappeared out the door in a swirl of embarrassed skirts.

Patrick let her go unchecked. He had done what he'd needed to ensure she would not be invading his space. Had he tried to send her away, she would have protested, but he couldn't have guaranteed her virtue if he had let her stay to tend him. The events of the last two days had weakened his control, and something about her pulled at the strands still holding it together.

Sighing, Patrick sat down to the meal Kathryn had left for him—stew, with a chunk of crusty bread slathered in butter. He looked over his burn as he dug in. It would need a good cleaning and wrapping, but the wound was in no danger of souring. Burns were commonplace for dragons, and this one would heal just as nicely as the rest of the burns he'd received.

He dropped his arm and glanced towards his now-shut door. Tomorrow, when he had collected his scattered control, he would thank Kathryn for both the meal and her concern. He would also have to think of an appropriate apology. He wanted some distance between them, but not a chasm he couldn't breach. Patrick let his mind wander to the feel of her in his arms, her sweet smell, and he imagined what her lips would taste like. For tonight, he would revel in her memory and dream of how good they could be together. Tomorrow, he would take up the mantle of protector of maidens and stay as far away from her temptation as he could.

Two planks of solid wood and a corridor separated them, but Kathryn didn't think it was enough as she leaned against her closed door. She could beat Daniel for suggesting she take that man something to eat and check on his wounds. She had only asked if he was okay because he had slept all day. Wounds such as his could fester if not treated properly. The first sign of souring was a tired patient, so she did have cause to worry.

Kathryn looked around her freshly cleaned room as she thought. Her eyes landed on the bundle of wildflowers she had gathered while they were out waiting for the sheets to dry. She had meant to take them to Patrick to sweeten his chambers, but she had forgotten them in her worry. Taking them to him now was out of the question.

Blushing, she remembered his touch. So warm and strong against her. Kathryn pushed away from the door and went to the flowers. They smelled sweet, but they did nothing to clean her mind of the scent of her new lord. *Oh, he smelled good. Musky and spicy.* Just the thought of it warmed her insides in a way she never knew was possible. Plucking up the bouquet of flowers, she cracked open her door. His door was

68

shut, and no one was in the corridor. She quickly secured the bundle to his door handle and fled back to her room. Surely he would find them there and take them inside.

What should she do now? Kathryn pondered her situation. She should be indignant. Hadn't her lord just suggested she pay for his service with her body? But she found that she wasn't. Her mind kept remembering the feel of his body against hers, his warm breath on her face, and the closeness of his lips. *What would it be like to kiss him?* She almost wished she had closed that gap and found out. No one had ever held her like that before, and she couldn't think of anyone she had ever wanted to hold her like that. Her mind churned on the possibilities, and she quickly shook them away. She shouldn't be thinking of romancing this man. There were nine girls she had to think about. How was she to expect them to keep their virtue when she was thinking about discarding her own?

No, she couldn't think of Patrick that way. He was their lord and protector, but he was also a slacker. Hadn't he left his men in Daniel's care so he could sleep the day away? Yes, that was it. It didn't matter if he had been severely rattled and burned, he should have been up seeing to his keep and hunting the dragon. Kathryn nodded her head and stormed out of her room, determined to be mad at him. Better mad than that other emotion swirling around and making her want to find out exactly how well they fit together.

Chapter Five

"THE MEN HAVE A NEW LIMERICK." DANIEL DROPPED himself to the seat next to Patrick.

Patrick sighed. "Surely not." He pushed the food around in his bowl. The great hall was bustling with activity this morning.

"Oh, yes." Daniel smiled and snatched up a biscuit from the table. "Would you like to hear it?"

"Is there any way to stop you?"

The grin on Daniel's face widened. "No."

Patrick sighed again. "Then let's have it."

Daniel cleared his throat as if he were going to announce the rhyme to the whole room.

Patrick cringed in anticipation.

"There once was a dragon named Patrick, whose scales and wings were fantastic. He soared through the air, with the greatest of care, and made all of the villagers spastic." Daniel spoke in a voice just loud enough for Patrick to hear.

Shock filled Patrick's face. "Spastic!" he hissed.

71

"Surely they overreacted by sending the maidens here, but it wasn't *that* bad."

Daniel chuckled. "There have been no less than five dragon sightings since yesterday," he said as if he were proud of that fact.

"*Five!*" Patrick snapped. He was going to have to crack some heads if they were showing themselves so openly.

Another laugh bubbled out of Daniel. "One was a cat in a tree, three were leaves in the wind, and one was a very ferocious-looking bush." He drew in a deep breath, sobering up. "I've had to send more men out to the village to check on these claims. The people are seeing dragons everywhere now."

Great. And entirely his fault. Drawing in a deep breath, Patrick ruffled his hand through his hair, thinking. "The people will calm down after a few days." He prayed that was true. "We'll just have to wait them out. Have the men continue to check into these claims to reassure the village. In the meantime, I want no one in wings." Lifting up his head, he gave Daniel a serious look. "We can't afford to panic the people more."

"But what about the search for the dragon?" Daniel asked.

Patrick sighed. "It will have to be done on horse." It would take them longer, but his scouts were good.

They would locate the dragon's lair. They had to.

"I'll pass on the word." Daniel bit into his biscuit. This was not going to make the men happy.

"*The dragon is back!*" The words echoed around the great hall as the doors banged open. Everyone froze for a moment before exploding into action.

Leaping from his seat, Patrick raced to the guard panting by the door. "Where is it?" He had to yell over the din to be heard.

The man pointed towards the door. "In the field to the south of the village. The men were just forming up their line when I left."

"My sword." Patrick turned back so he could go get his weapons.

A young girl held his sword for him. "Here, My Lord."

He looked at the weapon. It was definitely the one he had left in his room. *How had she known where to get it?* Stunned, he took it with a quick word of thanks. He didn't have time to worry about that now. Belting the sword to his waist, he ran out the door.

"My Lord!"

Patrick turned at the title. He was starting to get used to it. A bucket of cold water splashed into his face, driving the air from his lungs. Another spilled down his back, drenching his clothing. He should have expected that. A third hit him in the chest. Now they were just goofing off. He opened his mouth to snap at the men. The water was needed, but they should have given him at least a *little* warning.

"My Lord." The soft voice cut through his ire, and the bucket wielders beat a hasty retreat as Kathryn distracted him.

He stilled as she stepped close to him.

She reached for his hand and placed something in it. "Here."

Looking down, he discovered two smoke packs—smoke packs he distinctly remembered giving to Daniel. He raised his free hand and curled it over hers. The feel of her delicate hand in his made his blood warm. The noise around him fell away as he looked into her blue eyes. Their color had deepened with fright laced with a touch of desire. Oh, how he longed for an opportunity to push that fear from her heart. "Thank you." He breathed the words as he caressed her hand. Her breath caught in her throat, making her bosom swell slightly. Just one step would bring him close enough to pull her in for a kiss. His foot moved of its own accord, but the cry of a horse cut through his desire, and the sounds of the world came rushing back in.

"My Lord."

Patrick turned his head to see two men waiting

for him. One held his horse and the other his battered shield. He hadn't had time to repair it, but it would be better than nothing.

"Be safe, My Lord." Kathryn stepped away, pulling free of his hand. A blush kissed her cheeks.

So she had been affected, too. He smiled to himself before turning to his men. Grabbing the oversized shield, he leaped onto the bare back of his horse. Thankfully, someone had taken the time to bridle the animal. He kicked into its sides, sending it racing towards the town. Once he had subdued the dragon again, he would be back to pursue his fair maiden.

Fear clenched at her heart as Kathryn watched her lord gallop away. Several other men joined him in his haste, but her eyes followed Patrick. She tried to tell herself that the fear was for the village, but she knew that was not the case. She worried her lower lip with her teeth. It had taken every ounce of self-control to keep from begging him to stay. She couldn't bear the thought of him being injured by the dragon again.

A warmth at her side drew Kathryn's attention from the retreating party.

Lillian stood next to her, watching the men. "Do

you like him?"

"Of course not," Kathryn answered flippantly.

"Then why do you look so forlorn?"

Kathryn turned widened eyes to the other maiden. *Am I that transparent?* "I worry for the safety of our lord and his men," Kathryn answered as she turned back towards the castle.

"Of course," Lillian said sarcastically.

"Our continuing security depends on them winning this day," Kathryn pointed out.

"So your countenance has nothing to do with our good lord Mylan?" The way Lillian said that made Kathryn pause and look at her. There was a suggestion there that the older woman did not like.

"Of course not," Kathryn snapped. "Come on." She turned to stride purposefully into the great hall. "There is much to do before they return."

And there was. The chaos of the men's departure had left the great hall in shambles. It would take them a while to set it right.

Sliding from the horse, Patrick slapped the beast on the rump, sending it back to the castle. It was smart. It would find its way home. Hefting his battered shield, he loped towards the line of men formed up outside the south edge of town.

The dragon paced the field where they had first stood off.

"Report!" Patrick barked as he came to the line.

The creature's head turned at the sound of his voice.

"It landed a few minutes ago," one of his men answered. "It's been pacing back and forth, but it hasn't advanced on the village."

Nodding, Patrick watched the dragon. *What was it waiting for?*

The creature pinned him with its eyes.

"What are you going to do?" Daniel asked as he stepped up behind Patrick. They had talked about ways to kill the beast if it attacked the village again, but this wasn't attacking. How could he kill a creature for just showing up?

Patrick stepped through the line of men and out into the field. "Find out what it wants."

He stopped about halfway to the dragon and considered it.

The dragon cocked its head the other way and considered him.

"*Dragon!*" Patrick yelled. "Have you come to surrender?" *One could always hope.*

Pawing the ground, the creature scraped deep furrows in the dirt with his claws. "Maidens," the thing growled in a voice that was almost too guttural to understand.

If this creature had ever had a human side, it was long out of touch with it.

"There are no maidens here," Patrick yelled back.

The dragon growled and shot him an accusing stare.

What the hell did it think he had done to the maidens?

"Maidens," it growled again.

"There are no maidens here," Patrick explained. "They're safe in my castle."

The creature extended its long neck and looked up at the large, stone structure.

"Don't even think about it," Patrick growled.

Drawing in a few deep breaths, the dragon stoked its fires. Smoke trickled out of its nose as it turned its attention back to Patrick. "*Maidens*," it rumbled again.

"*No*," Patrick yelled, "you may not have the maidens." He clenched his shield, ready for the attack he could see coming.

Digging its claws into the ground again, the dragon lowered its head and spread out its wings. It thrashed its tail and let out a mighty roar in challenge.

Patrick threw his hands back, bent forwards at the waist, and answered with a roar of his own. His human voice was nothing compared to the echoing sound of the dragon, but he put all of his heart into it. Just the fact that the beast had landed in the field showed it held respect for Patrick's claim on the town. He would meet this challenge with whatever it took to defend that claim. "The maidens are mine, and you shall not have them!" Patrick screamed.

Desperation filled the creature's eyes as it pawed the ground franticly. "Maidens." There was a note of begging in the creature's voice. There was something not right about this. What could drive a dragon to beg?

"No." Patrick stood firm in his decision. He could not let this creature kill any more people.

The dragon snorted at him before kicking into the air and taking flight.

Patrick spun back to face his men. "Find horse and follow it!" he yelled. "I want the lair found *now!*" That thing inside him that didn't sit right with his dragon was screaming at him now. There was more going on here than he knew.

"On horses?" Daniel asked as he met Patrick coming back. The best answer would be to shift to dragon and follow it.

"Yes, on horses," Patrick answered. "With the people seeing dragons in every shadow, we can't afford to set after it on wings." He turned his head to catch Daniel's eyes. "Did you see it?"

Daniel swallowed as he nodded. "Yes." He had noticed the tension in the dragon. What could cause such distress?

"I have to take this to the prince tonight. Something isn't right."

Daniel nodded his agreement.

"We *have* to find that dragon's lair," Patrick stressed.

"We will do our best, My Lord." Daniel placed his fist over his heart and bowed before breaking off to order the men around.

The weight of Daniel's words hit Patrick, and his shoulders dropped as he turned to walk back to the castle. Great, now his friend was seeing him as the lord he was trying to be. Guess that meant he was doing a fair job. The fact that he was claiming the place as lord hadn't sunken in until Daniel had used the title.

Patrick could feel the eyes of the villagers as he passed. Each one added weight to his shoulders. He had claimed them, he had defended them, and he was now responsible for them. They expected him to kill this dragon, but in his heart, he knew there was something wrong. The dragon needed help, but what could it need maidens for?

Drawing in a deep breath, Patrick straightened

his spine. He had come into this situation knowing he would be the lord here. He just hadn't realized how heavy that burden would be.

"You're back."

Daniel's voice echoing down the hall made Kathryn pause. *What was he doing up this late at night?* It was well into the wee hours of the morning.

"Yes," Patrick's voice answered. "The light in the tower was very helpful. Thank you."

Kathryn sucked in a shocked breath. She had tried to take the lord dinner this evening, but Daniel had sent her away, claiming Patrick was tired and had gone to bed. *What was he doing up now, and where had he gone?* Kathryn eased herself down the hall, listening to the men.

"The robe was a nice touch," Patrick's voice went on.

Kathryn peeked around the corner at the two men. Patrick wore a long dressing gown.

Daniel shrugged. "I figured that would be better than running around a castle filled with maidens naked. How did your trip go?"

"Well," Patrick answered. "It's a beautiful night for flying."

What did he mean flying? Kathryn's brow furrowed in thought.

"And what did the prince say?" Daniel asked.

Prince? There was no prince here. Patrick's answer was cut off as the two men disappeared into Patrick's room. Kathryn paused as her mind repeated the conversation she had just heard. *What was going on?*

Shaking her thoughts away, Kathryn hastened to her room. Her door was right across the hall from where the two men had disappeared, and she needed to get into it before they came back out and discovered her eavesdropping. Her hand dropped to the handle of her door. *Safe.*

"Kathryn?"

Daniel's voice froze her. She twisted to look at him, trying to hide the fear in her eyes.

"Master Daniel!" she gasped in surprise. She hadn't heard the other door open.

"What are you doing up so late?" He closed the distance between them.

Oh God, she was in for it now. "Dinner wasn't sitting well," she explained as she tried to keep the panicked expression from her face. "I was just coming back from the garderobes."

Daniel considered her for a moment. "I have some mint tea that would help settle your stomach," he offered. "Would you like me to fetch it?"

Kathryn bit the inside of her cheek. Could she be lucky enough to get out of this unscathed? "Thank you, but no," she refused. "My stomach is much better now. I'm hoping I can get back to sleep for a while longer."

Daniel held her gaze as if he were searching her face for the truth. "Rest easy then, fair maiden." He reached around her and opened her door.

She stepped past him and into her room. "Thank you, Master Daniel."

Daniel nodded his farewell and pulled the door shut behind her.

Leaning against the closed door, she listened to his footfalls take him away. *Thank you, God.* She let out a sigh of relief as she shucked her dressing gown and slipped back into her bed. Her mind replayed the last few minutes as she tried to get comfortable.

Patrick had obviously not gone to bed this evening, so why had Daniel lied to her? And where had Patrick gone? The comment about flying nagged at her. *How could one fly?* She could only think of one creature large enough to carry a man. Kathryn's heart skipped a beat. *Could their new lord be in cohorts with the dragon?* Tales of him yelling at the dragon had come back with the men. *No, he wouldn't align himself with such a creature.* She shook that thought away.

Rolling over, Kathryn thought about the rest of the conversation. *Why would Patrick be wandering around the castle naked?* She was sure she'd heard Daniel say that, and he'd been wearing a dressing gown. *Maybe he had just gotten up to use the garderobes, too?* She shook her head. No, he had come from the direction of the tower. *What were they doing up in the tower this late at night?*

Memories tickled at the back of her brain. Something her grandmother had said. Kathryn's mouth fell open as old stories flooded her mind, stories of an age long past, when dragons had learned to walk as men. They lived and prospered together until the men had become jealous and frightened of the dragons. Her grandmother had spoken of a great purge, when all the dragons had been hunted down and killed.

Obviously, one had escaped. *Could there have been more?* The image of a red dragon bursting from the lake filled her mind. *Could Patrick be a dragon?* It would definitely explain a few things. Like how he'd been able to face down the black dragon twice without being eaten or cooked. He had also claimed to know a few things about dragons, and he said he'd used dragon's fire to forge his shield. Daniel had also made a comment about the dragon's fire being nearly as hot as Patrick's.

Kathryn rolled to her other side as she worked

on this. Patrick had to be a dragon in human guise. It was the only answer that made sense. The question now was, what should she do about it? Patrick had said not all dragons were bad. *Did that mean he was good?* He had stopped the black dragon from terrorizing the town, and he had accepted the maidens into his protection. *Was he only biding his time and earning their trust before striking? Did he eat maidens, too?* Kathryn paused on that thought. *Why* did *the dragon eat maidens? Did they taste better than those who were not?* She shuddered at the thought and went back to wondering what to do about Patrick.

If he were a dragon, how could she find out? Was there a spell he used to change forms? Would he tell her if she asked? Would she dare to ask him? No, she would never dare to ask him. She could easily guess the reasons he would hide his true self. In their fright, the townspeople might act in haste. Her grandmother had told of mobs taking dragons to be drawn and quartered. She couldn't bear the thought of Patrick being torn limb from limb.

Kathryn rolled into her blankets again. No, she would not pry into his life. His secrets were better left alone.

Six

DANIEL RAISED AN EYEBROW AT PATRICK AS THEY STARED at the dragon just outside their main gate. "What do you think?"

Turning away from the sight, Patrick climbed down from the battlement. "Get the men to saddle their horses. I want them to follow him as soon as he leaves." He hated to send the men out on horseback, but the village's response to dragon sightings made it impossible for the men to safely shift.

Pushing the main gate open, Patrick walked out to stand in the center of the road. Having asserted his dominance over the dragon yesterday, he left his shield behind as a show of trust.

There was that same considering cock to the dragon's head.

"What can I do for you?" Patrick called calmly to the beast. It was obvious the creature wanted something.

"Maidens," it growled.

86

"No." Patrick held his hands wide. "You may not have my maidens."

A threat rumbled up from the dragon's chest.

Patrick growled right back at him.

The dragon's eyes narrowed. It dipped its head and lifted it up, quickly opening its jaws. Something arced through the air and landed near Patrick's feet. Gold coins spilled out across the ground.

"Maidens," it growled again.

The contents of the bag shocked Patrick. *Was it trying to buy the women?* He bent over and picked up the treasure. "These women are not for sale." He slid the coins back into the leather satchel and held it out for the dragon to take.

The dragon thumped its tail on the ground in frustration. "*Maidens!*" it roared.

"*No!*" Patrick roared back. "You cannot have the maidens!" He dropped his hand down to his side. The dragon had made no move to take the gold back, and the bag was heavy. "Tell me what is wrong, and I will see what I can do to help."

The dragon's massive head wove back and forth in despair. "*Maidens.*" This time the word came out as almost a whimper.

It broke Patrick's heart to refuse again, but he did. This creature was in pain and desperate. He needed something from a maiden but couldn't com-

87

municate what it was.

The creature whimpered, pawed the ground, and took to the skies, leaving Patrick with the bag of gold.

"Find him!" Patrick cried as soon as he was back inside the gates. Men galloped past him, chasing after the dragon as he looked down at the satchel of gold. For a dragon to willingly part with this much treasure was unheard of. *Why did he need maidens so badly that he was willing to pay for them?* Especially if he had gone as feral as he seemed. "We have to find his lair."

Patrick looked up as Daniel came to him. "This is not right." He tossed the bag of gold to the other man.

Daniel hefted it, feeling its weight. "No. It's not." Shock rode in his eyes. He fell into step with Patrick as they headed towards the castle.

"Have we discovered anything?"

Daniel shrugged. "Only that he disappears into the forests towards the south, which border the mountains. There's the possibility of a cave system or a narrow valley there. But wherever he's going, he keeps it well hidden. He goes miles out of his way to lose the scouts. Douglas thinks he shifts to a lesser form before doubling back to his lair."

That thought was outrageous. Patrick shook his head, bewildered. "But feral dragons don't shift."

"I didn't think so, either, but how can something that size continue to elude us?"

Patrick nodded. Daniel did have a point there. "We might have to go after it in wings."

Daniel agreed.

"If we don't find him today and he comes back tomorrow, have the men prepared to go out again. Once they reach the forest and are well away from prying eyes, I want the five smallest to shift and search. Maybe they can smell him out. The rest will do their best on horseback. We'll set the brazier in the tower alight so the scouts can find their way back once the sun has set. It should be safer to fly over at night."

Smacking his fist into his chest, Daniel nodded. "Yes, My Lord."

Reaching out, Patrick grabbed the man's arm before he could take off to spread the word. "And, Daniel?" He pulled him to a stop and gave his friend a confused look. "Am I doing the right thing?" Patrick could feel Daniel size him up as he measured the weight of the bag once more.

"This dragon has killed many, and for that he must answer," he held the gold out for Patrick to take back, "but there is something more to this story than what we are seeing. The orders we were given were to stop a rogue dragon from terrorizing this village.

Since we have arrived, he has neither razed nor killed. So, yes. You are doing the right thing. Once we find this dragon, we can bring its problem to the prince. He can decide what to do from there."

Patrick cradled the sack of gold and nodded. It felt good to have someone else confirm his thoughts. Now all he had to do was find this dragon. But, first, he had to find a good place to store the dragon's treasure until he could return it.

Patrick pushed his chamber door open with a heavy sigh. It had been a long day. Most of the scouts had already returned empty-handed. The dragon had disappeared into the woods as if by magic.

Patrick paused. *Maybe it was using magic to hide itself.* That might explain why they had been so unsuccessful. He'd have to have Daniel send some of the men who could see through spells tomorrow.

"Good evening, My Lord."

The soft voice broke into his thoughts. His eyes found a woman sitting at his table. The fire had died to embers, casting the girl in flickering shadows. He drew in a breath, scenting the air. He knew this girl. "Lillian?' Patrick asked.

Lillian stood up so the light shone in her golden

hair. She had done something to it to emphasize the curls. Her form-fitting dress pushed her bosom up to an almost indecent level. "At your service, My Lord." She dropped a low curtsy, showing off her chest. Her movement left almost nothing to his imagination.

Moving to the hearth, he dropped a few more logs on the fire to brighten the room. "What are you doing here?" He did not like being in such a dark place with her alone.

"I've come to check on your wounds."

He glanced down at his arm, then back up to her face. Something about her eyes set him on edge. "Did Daniel put you up to this?" Daniel had been sending Kathryn after him since the women had arrived. Was he trying to tempt him with another woman now?

Lillian closed the distance between them slowly. "I came of my own accord." She moved with an alluring grace that spoke of things maidens should not know.

He stilled as she approached.

Her hand reached out to take up his wounded arm. "I wanted to make sure my lord was taken care of." Lillian rested his hand on her chest above her heart. "I also wanted to thank you for protecting us." The look in her eyes spoke of desire but lacked the fear usually found in a maiden's eyes.

Patrick's jaw clenched as she stepped in against

him.

"Is there anything I can do for you?" Her hand came up to caress his cheek in an attempt to bring his lips down where she could reach them. "Anything at all?"

Oh, this was no maiden!

Kathryn balanced the heavy tray in her arms as she stepped through the open door to Patrick's room. "Pardon me, My Lord. Daniel sent me to dress your wounds."

She froze as she took in the shocking scene. Lillian was caught in Patrick's embrace. One hand caressed the skin above her heart as the other held on to her upper arm. Pain ripped at Kathryn's heart. "Forgive me," she cried on the edge of tears.

How could she have been so foolish as to let her heart soften to him? Hadn't she learned anything from the first time Daniel had sent her to tend his wound? He was nothing but a rogue, there to steal maidens' virtues away and leave them brokenhearted.

As she spun to leave, the tray filled with supplies caught on the edge of the door and slipped from her hand. It crashed to the ground with the sound of shattering glass. She might as well have thrown her heart on the floor. "I'm sorry." Leaving the mess, she turned and ran out. She couldn't stand to be in the castle one more second. Not after catching the man she just realized she loved holding another.

Patrick could hear the tears in Kathryn's words as she raced away. Her heart breaking was almost as audible as the jar of salve that had crashed on his floor.

Turning his attention back to the wanton woman in his grasp, he finished shoving her away. "I want nothing from you. Leave." Turning on his heels, he raced after the woman he did want. He would deal with Lillian later.

"Kathryn!" Shouting after her, Patrick ran down the corridor. He saw the hem of her dress disappear around the corner leading to the great hall. Man, she could move when she wanted to.

Bursting into the hall, he paused until his eyes caught her skirting around the end of the tables, heading for the main door. Ignoring the men who were still having dinner, Patrick leaped onto the table and ran across it, closing some of the distance between them. *Oh, there would be rhymes about this tomorrow!* But he didn't care.

Kathryn was halfway down the steps by the time he made it to the door. She'd grabbed up her skirts and was taking the steps three at a time. Without anything in her way, she had really poured her heart into her flight.

Kicking up his heels, Patrick bounded down after her. The thrill of the chase had heated his blood. She was fast, but he was faster. She had only gotten a few yards from the steps when his arms closed around her, halting her flight.

"*No!*" Screaming, she stomped her foot down on his, trying to get away from him.

Patrick turned her in his arms and kissed her hard on the lips, crushing her to him. Even in his excited state, he remembered how he could affect a woman. He kissed her passionately, but he kept it shallow.

Under the caress of his lips, the fight washed out of Kathryn, and she went nearly limp in his arms.

"*Shhhh.*" Soothing her, he shifted his hand into her dark locks to turn her face into the crook of his neck. He supported her as she clenched her fingers into the front of his shirt and sobbed uncontrollably. "I'm here." Patrick kissed the hair at the side of her head.

Anger drove her to struggle in his arms, but his hold was unrelenting.

94

He shushed her again as he held on, waiting for her to calm.

"I saw… I saw…" She stuttered, sobbing too hard to speak.

"You saw me caught in an unwanted advance," Patrick whispered softly as he nuzzled her hair. "She came to me, but I turned her away."

Kathryn drew in a sniffling breath.

He kept a light hold on her in case she decided to run again, but he let loose of her head so she could lean back and look up into his face. Her eyes were rimmed with red, and her skin had gone all blotchy. She was definitely not a dainty crier, but he couldn't help but smile at her. The fact that she wasn't perfect at this made it that much more endearing.

"I want no other." He pressed a soft kiss to her lips before leaning back to look into her eyes. Through the tears, he could see her desire, as well as the fear that marked her as a maiden.

She sniffled. "Truly?"

Patrick threw back his head and let out a laugh as he squeezed her tighter to him. "I just ran across the dinner table for you." He smiled. "A feat I'm not likely to live down anytime soon."

She looked slightly appalled.

He pressed another light kiss to her lips before cuddling her to him. "And I would venture to guess half the castle is standing behind me on the steps as we speak," he whispered into her ear.

The color drained from her face as she glanced over his shoulder to the crowd staring at them. He chuckled as she buried her face into his shoulder in embarrassment.

He glanced past her to the rest of the crowd on the castle grounds. "And the rest are here in the bailey." No matter how much he should, there was no denying his feelings now. Everyone would hear about this before dawn. "Come." Patrick pushed Kathryn away to stand on her own. At least her face was no longer blotchy from crying. It was bright red with humiliation.

Folding her hand over his good arm, he gave her an encouraging smile. "You still have a wound to dress." He held his hurt arm up to show her. The bandage hung loose where it had been pulled away in her struggles. Guiding her towards the castle, the crowd parted to let them back into the hall. Eyes followed them as they took a more leisurely route around the tables. He distinctly remembered there being a part in the middle of those tables when they had first arrived. Whoever had decided to push them together was going to get an earful when he found them.

Patrick glanced around the quiet room. They

were probably waiting for him to confess his love to her, as if chasing her through the castle weren't enough. But he couldn't give her words of undying affection yet. There was much they needed to discuss before he could give his heart to her. Dragons mate for life.

…And there was that one, little issue of him being a mythical, shape-shifting being that might give her reason to rethink her feelings. Yes, they definitely needed to talk.

"I'm sorry." Kathryn's hand slipped from Patrick's arm as soon as they reached his room. Lillian was gone, but there was still a mess in his doorway. Dropping to her knees, she started to gather the things she had dropped in her hasty retreat. She could feel Patrick's eyes on her, so she kept her head down and her hands busy with her task. She didn't know what to feel.

A jumble of emotions swirled through her. Her heart still hurt at the memory of Lillian in Patrick's arms, her body burned with desire from his kisses, and she was mortified that she had made them both look like fools in front of the whole castle. To top it all off, he'd said he wanted her, but he hadn't said he loved her. She sniffed back the tears she felt burning at the corner of her eyes.

Patrick sighed behind her. "It's all right." His hands smoothed down her upper arms, caressing her. "I do care about you." His fingers caught her elbows, and he lifted her to her feet. She sniffled again as he pulled her back against him and circled her with his arms. "I have for a while now." His breath was warm on the side of her face as he held her.

She closed her eyes, enjoying the feel of him. They fit together so perfectly. *Too perfectly.* There was going to be something to keep them apart—Kathryn just knew it. He talked of caring, but not of love. *Was there another? Was he married? Was he really a dragon?* She tensed in his arms, waiting for the other shoe to drop.

"Kathryn."

Here it comes.

"I care for you, and I want no other, but there is more to me than what you see. I can't just give my heart to anyone. There are things you need to know."

Kathryn held her breath, waiting for it. She felt Patrick draw in a ragged breath.

"The woman I choose is not in for an easy life. I'm the adopted son of King Mylan."

And there it was. He was royal. She blew out her breath. So, it was her station in life he had an issue with. She felt her ire rise, burning through the hurt. "I see," she said, embracing the anger and stepping forward, breaking his hold on her. "So I'm not good enough for you."

"What?" Patrick asked.

Was that shock in his voice? Oh, he was *good.* He would woo her, ravage her, and then leave her. Her anger peaked. "I think I understand now," she snapped as she turned on him.

Patrick backed up under her fury.

"I am not a toy. I have a heart and feelings, and I will not let you play with me!"

He took another step back. "*What?*"

"Good night, Lord Mylan." With that, Kathryn turned and stormed out of his room. She would have preferred to leave the castle entirely, but going back out past all those people was out of the question. She had already embarrassed herself enough.

Slamming her door, she locked it before dropping herself onto her bed to cry. *First impressions are always right*, she chided herself. She should never have softened her heart to him. He was nothing but a self-serving, pompous ass.

Patrick stared at Kathryn's door, trying to figure out what had just happened. He had brought her back to lay out his life for her, and she had stormed away before he had even gotten started. What had he said to upset her? He ran both his hands through his hair, ruffling it up. Maybe if he got more blood up there, his brain would work better.

"What did you do?" Daniel asked as he looked from Patrick's befuddled face to Kathryn's closed door.

"I have no idea," he admitted, looking to his friend as if he might explain the inner workings of women to him. "I was going to tell her, but she stormed off before I could."

Pausing, Daniel considered him. "You love her that much?"

"She plagues my every waking thought and haunts my dreams." Patrick leaned against his door-jamb, staring at Kathryn's closed door.

Daniel grinned at him. "And here I thought you were avoiding her."

"I *was*," Patrick snapped, "but you kept sending her to tempt me!" Turning back into his room, he kicked the tray of supplies Kathryn had dropped.

Chuckling, Daniel came in and shut the door. "If I didn't know better, I would say you were brood-ing."

"I haven't had a brooding in over ten years," Patrick snapped again. He dropped himself into a chair and glared at Daniel.

"Oh yes, definitely brooding."

Patrick glared harder at him.

"You're moody, impulsive, and unpredictable. Love can do that to you."

"How can I be in love?" Patrick growled. "I've only known her for a few days."

"Instinct, my good man." Daniel snickered. "Your dragon knows what it wants and will give you trouble until you let your heart follow."

Patrick let out a deep sigh. "Fine," he grumbled. There was no way logic would win out against instinct. That had been tried, and it led to some crazed dragons. "So what do I do about her?" He was more than willing to give in, but it was convincing the girl that was turning into an issue.

"That, my friend, is the biggest mystery of all." Daniel grinned. "Figure out the mind of a woman, and you could be the wealthiest man in the world."

"What do I do about her?" This time Patrick's voice held a note of pleading.

Daniel sighed and brushed his fingers through his hair. "Let her calm down for the night," he offered. "Try again tomorrow."

"What if she won't talk to me?"

"Then I'll talk to her. Just let it be for now. Tend

your wound and try to get some rest." Patrick opened his mouth to protest, but Daniel cut him off with a raised hand. "If you can't sleep, go take a flight. It will ease you mind and help you work things out."

Patrick nodded. That was a great idea. Being in scales would clear his rational mind so he could sort through the conflicting emotions. Then tomorrow, with his head on straight, he would face Kathryn and clear up whatever misunderstanding they were having.

Seven

SHAKING HIS HEAD, PATRICK WATCHED THE DRAGON fly away again. The creature had returned with a larger bag of gold, demanding maidens, and he had turned it away again. What else could he do?

The scouts had ridden out to the edge of the forest at sunrise so they would be ready in dragon form to follow the creature when it returned. They had to find the lair soon. The dragon was getting more desperate, and Patrick could not think of anything that would make him want maidens.

The day was not turning out well. Kathryn was avoiding him. He'd seen her across the hall at breakfast but had been stopped with a question before he could reach her. When he was done, she was gone. He had tried to ask where she went, but the other maidens were giving him the cold shoulder as well.

The morning had been a disaster. At breakfast, his porridge was cold, his cheese was moldy, and his bread was soggy. There was even horsehair in his drink! Giving up, he had gone back to his room to find someone had doused his fire and stolen the wood from his hearth. Grumbling, he'd dropped himself down across his bed to regroup but found that, too, had been watered. Thank goodness he hadn't used the chamber pot in the night. They might have used that instead.

After getting back up, he changed his shirt and went to find something he could do in the bailey. Most of the rubble had been cleared, but the men were working on rebuilding the stables and store-rooms. Surely they could use a hand.

No such luck. Two groups turned him away, claiming he couldn't work with his burned arm, and a third group snapped and growled at him enough that he just left. Everyone seemed to be mad at him for what he'd said to Kathryn, but no one would tell him why she was upset!

The only useful thing he had done was turn the dragon away, but even that had gotten him scorn-ful looks. Apparently, the maidens had taken offense when he'd claimed them as his. *Great!*

No one in the castle would let him help. He couldn't forge his shield anew without turning drag-on. He couldn't find Kathryn to clear up their mis-understanding. Even his horse had attempted to take a chunk out of him when he'd tried to clean a rock from its shoe. Everything was starting to make him grouchy and bitter. Seeing the downhill slide, Patrick grabbed some field rations and two flagons of mead and went to find a place where no one would look.

"There you are."

Patrick cracked a very drunken eye at the voice. He knew to whom it belonged, but the name wouldn't come to him at the moment. Scowling, he raised the second skin of mead to his lips. The first lay empty next to his untouched food.

"Do you know how long I've been looking for you?" the man asked as he sat down next to Patrick.

Rolling his head over, Patrick considered the man, but answering the question took too much brainpower, so he just shrugged.

"A long time." The man took the skin from Patrick's hand and took a long pull of the mead.

"Hey!" Patrick protested. His brow furrowed as he made his brain work. "Gif tat bak… Danel," he slurred.

Laughing, Daniel took another pull of the mead. "You, my friend, are well and truly soused." He capped the flagon and set it out of Patrick's reach. "How long have you been up here?"

Patrick shrugged. It's not like anyone cared that he had squirreled himself away. The castle had probably run better without him anyway.

Daniel sighed. "I've been in every nook and cranny of this castle from the dungeon to the tallest tower, and if Mathew hadn't mentioned seeing movement up here when he flew over, I would still be looking," he said, exasperated. "I didn't even know this tower had a door in it."

Patrick had found his way up to the top of one of the smaller towers. "Shood'v gonn hep," he slurred.

"What?" Daniel asked.

"Shood hev gotn hep." He tried again, but his tongue was too thick.

"I should have gotten help?" Daniel questioned.

Patrick nodded, making his friend laugh.

"Help! I couldn't get anyone to volunteer. And the men I *did* order to find you might have spent maybe ten minutes walking through the main rooms of the castle before coming back and telling me you weren't here. I thought you might have gone out for a ride, but your horse was still in the bailey."

"Mmm bit me," Patrick grumbled.

"He bit you?" Daniel asked.

Patrick nodded and leaned over against Daniel's shoulder. "Nuun wats me." He sounded so pathetic. He had been up here for hours, and the castle hadn't exploded. In fact, it had probably run better under Daniel's supervision. Just that thought had Patrick sliding further down into depression. He wasn't just unwanted, he was also unneeded.

Daniel sighed. "Of course we want you, Patrick." He was starting to get the hang of Patrick's drunken ramblings.

So, the depression part of brooding had set in. Of all the things Patrick could have come up with for getting wasted, not being wanted was a poor excuse. He was, after all, supposed to be the lord of the castle.

Patrick just shook his head pathetically.

"How do you think Kathryn would feel seeing you like this?" Daniel asked, trying to reach him through the alcohol.

"Sheee dunt car," Patrick nearly sobbed. "Hats mme."

Daniel tried to keep the grin off his face. This really shouldn't be funny, but it was. "She doesn't hate you," he soothed. "You've had a misunderstanding that can easily be fixed if you would sit down and talk it out."

"Hats me." Patrick oozed over farther, making Daniel's grin widen.

"Oh, Patrick." He put his arm around his near-unconscious friend. "What the hell am I going to do with you?"

Gentle snores answered him.

Letting out a deep sigh, Daniel looked around. The first thing he needed to do was get the man down from here. He had picked a fine place to get smashed. The view was incredible, yet the wall Patrick leaned against hid him from anyone looking down from the tallest tower. Daniel knew. He had climbed up there to search for the missing man. Twice. The only access to this tower was through a small hatch in the back of one of the storerooms. A long, rickety ladder reached up through an aviary to the small rooftop. Apparently, someone in this castle had kept homing pigeons at one time.

There was an impressive drop to the bailey below. Patrick could probably have watched Daniel run around searching for him if he hadn't been wallowing in self-pity. It a good thing the man hadn't tried to get down after drinking himself silly. It would have made one hell of a mess if he had fallen, and that was not a conversation he wanted to have with Kyle. Not to mention what it would do to Kathryn.

As it was, she was probably going to feel guilty over this. Daniel had talked to her and found out what Patrick had said. He could see that she had taken Patrick's words wrong. She hadn't let him finish. Daniel tried to explain that there was more to the lord's story and she needed to hear him out. She had begrudgingly agreed to listen. That had been nearly six hours ago, when Daniel had begun his search.

Daniel looked up to the twinkling sky. Full night had fallen some time ago. That gave him an idea. A dragon would have no problem plucking them from the perch. He pulled Patrick around until he was lying flat on his back. He hated to leave the drunken man there by himself, but the landing was too small for him to shift.

"Be still," Daniel warned as he shimmied through the hole and down the ladder. All he had to do was slip out of the castle, shift, fly up here, collect Patrick, take him away from the grounds, and shift back without being seen. Cake! Then he could tote the drunken man's carcass in and say he found him in the woods. No one need be the wiser. Then, he was going to find someone to seal up that damned hole so this didn't happen again. *Bloody, brooding dragons!*

Kathryn sat in a ring of consoling faces as she pulled her needle through the hem of a new skirt. Several of the maidens had come to comfort her as she worked on her sewing by the fire's light. She had told no one of the way Patrick had shunned her the night before, but the castle had been abuzz with it this morning. Someone must have seen her come out of his chambers upset. It was amazing how fast gossip spread around the castle.

Throughout the day, Kathryn had received nothing but sympathy for her plight. She had barely avoided Patrick in the morning, but she managed to elude him throughout the day. At first, it lightened her heart to see so many giving the man a hard time, but as the day wore on, their actions bothered her. Why were they treating him so rottenly? True, he had broken her heart, but did his actions really deserve the level of scorn he was receiving? Did it have something to do with the very public display of affection followed so closely by him turning her away?

Kathryn gave pause to that thought. He really hadn't turned her away. Daniel pointed out that she had taken what Patrick had said and jumped to conclusions. Had she? It had taken her a while to see it, but she had. When Patrick had not declared his love for her, she was certain he would shun her, and she had grabbed at the first reason she could find to leave. It just so happened that his being royal put him far enough above her station that it really could be an issue. She had grabbed at that straw to defend her heart. Having realized her error, she had stopped hiding hours ago, but Patrick hadn't found her yet. He hadn't even come down for dinner. Maybe she should go find him?

"…force himself on you that way. The scoundrel should be beat." Camilla's voice broke into Kathryn's thoughts.

Kathryn reached out and grabbed her arm, interrupting the girl's rant. "What?"

"I said he should be beat," Camilla repeated. "He seemed so much better than that."

"Who seemed better?" Kathryn's heart froze; something was not right here.

"Lord Mylan. He doesn't seem the type to force himself on a maiden," Camilla explained. "And after such a display at dinner. I was completely shocked when he jumped up on the table."

"Camilla, who told you that Lord Mylan forced himself on me?" Her quiet voice made all the maidens with her stop working.

"I heard it from Bethany," Camilla said, pointing at the girl across from her.

"And you, Bethany?" Kathryn looked her way.

"I overheard Lillian telling Nana in the kitchen." Bethany looked confused.

Lillian! Anger boiled in Kathryn's gut. "What did Lillian say?"

Bethany looked around at the other faces for support, but they were all looking expectantly at her. "She said she saw Lord Mylan force you into his chambers." She swallowed hard before continuing. "She said he pushed you down in the doorway and fell on you. That you fought with him as he… as he…"

"As he *what?*" Kathryn pushed; she had an idea where this was going.

"Oh, Kathryn." Bethany bounced in her seat, frustrated that she was being forced into saying such a horrible thing. "She said he tried to take your maidenhood."

Kathryn stared at her, shocked.

"—That you fought him off and escaped into your room," Bethany continued, "and that the only reason he didn't break down your door was that Master Daniel came along and stopped him."

Things clicked into place. No wonder everyone was treating the man so poorly. They thought he had tried to force himself on her—a maiden he was sworn to protect.

"And you believed this?" The anger echoed through Kathryn's voice.

"We had no reason not to," Marlena answered from next to her.

Kathryn gave her a questioning look.

"You looked horrible this morning. You spent all day avoiding him, and when we asked if you wanted to talk about it, you said no."

Enlightenment dawned on Kathryn, and she nodded. "I see." She tried to keep her voice very level as she spoke. "Tell me something. Does Lord Mylan seem like a man who would accost a maiden?"

The girls looked at each other.

Bethany shook her head. "Not really."

"And do you think any man would try such a thing in an open doorway with a bed just a fathom away?"

The girls looked around at each other again.

"Only if he were desperate," Bethany answered again.

"Think carefully before you answer this next one." Kathryn's narrowed eyes held a strong warning in them. "Do you think a man who can stare down a dragon, without a shield, is desperate?"

"No," Bethany answered, her head bent in shame.

All the girls looked ashamed.

Kathryn's hands were clenched in anger. "I *did* have a disagreement with our good lord, but he did *not* hurt me. And he certainly never shoved me down."

This had to be Lillian's way of getting back at Patrick for refusing her. Such a rumor could be enough to destroy any man's reputation. "Have you all been passing this story around?" The looks on their faces told her all she needed to know. "I see."

How was she going to set this straight? Even if

she came out and told everyone the truth, the damage had been done. This wasn't the worst lie that she had ever heard, but it was obviously coloring everyone's view of the poor man. She would have to deal with Lillian.

The sound of the main door opening drew all of their attention.

"Master Daniel," Kathryn cried in surprise. It wasn't Daniel that shocked her. It was the view of the back end of a man over his shoulder that had her pushing her sewing from her lap and jumping up. "Is he…?" Kathryn's heart clenched at the possibilities. No one had seen Patrick for most of the day.

Daniel met her halfway around the table. "He's fine." He paused so she could turn Patrick's face to check on him. It was a little red from hanging upside down, but he seemed okay.

Kathryn ran her fingers through his hair, surprised by how soft it was. "Where did you find him?"

"He found himself an out-of-the-way spot with a skin or two of mead," Daniel explained. "Some rest will see him right."

She snorted with disgust. "Some Prince Charming."

Daniel laughed at her. "He may be many things, but a prince he is not."

Kathryn paused with her fingers tangled in Patrick's hair. "But, he said he was."

"He would never be so brazen," Daniel scoffed.

"He said he was the king's son," Kathryn countered.

Twisting around, he looked into her eyes. "He may have been raised by the queen, but he is no prince."

She cocked her head in question.

"This man's life is as complicated as he is heavy. Let me find a place to drop his sorry carcass, and I will explain." Daniel turned towards the door leading to the living space.

Having heard Kathryn's and Daniel's exchange, the maidens dropped their work and followed. The story of a would-be prince was something not to be missed.

Daniel sighed as half of the girls led the way and the rest followed.

"He's a prince?" Marlena asked.

Apparently, this explanation was not going to wait until he got Patrick back to his chambers. "No." Daniel shook his head. "He's an orphan the queen took in."

A murmur went through the girls.

"So, he *is* a prince," Bethany stated.

Daniel took a deep breath to keep from snapping at the women. "No," he said again. "Although the queen may call him son and the prince claims him as a brother, he lacks the bloodline to be a royal."

The women were quiet as they took this in.

Darkness met him as he pushed Patrick's door open. "Why's the fire out?" Daniel asked. He knew the man had been gone for most of the day, but there should still have been some embers left. The room was stone cold.

The girls were oddly silent.

"Never mind." He turned towards the bed. He could relight the fire once he had put Patrick down.

Kathryn skirted around him to pull the covers back. "Wait." She stopped as soon as she picked up the blanket.

Daniel paused as she reached her hand down to the mattress.

"This is wet." She rubbed her fingers over the soggy bedding.

Daniel could hear the maidens behind him shuffling their feet. No wonder Patrick was up in the tower drinking. A castle full of upset women could ruin anyone's day.

"My room." Kathryn turned to lead Daniel across the hall. More of the women had come out of their rooms to see what was going on. Spotting the one responsible, Kathryn altered her course.

Lillian didn't see Kathryn's hand move until it landed squarely on her cheek with a resonating crack.

"How *dare* you," Kathryn hissed.

Raising her hand to her stinging cheek, Lillian turned back to meet Kathryn's glare.

"First you come on to our lord like some wanton harlot, and then you besmirch his good name when he refuses you," Kathryn accused the younger woman.

A gasp circled through the maidens.

Daniel had been shocked when Kathryn had attacked the other woman without warning, but this left him flabbergasted. He knew something had occurred yesterday, but no one had been willing to share the rumors with him as he hunted for the missing lord. This went a long way to explaining why the man had gone on a drinking binge. He was going to have to have words with the men.

An evil smile turned the corner of Kathryn's mouth. "You should probably pack you things and go back to the village. If there's truth to the stories told by the baker's son, then you should have nothing to fear from a dragon looking for maidens."

Lillian's face turned bright red at the accusations. Screaming with rage, she launched herself at Kathryn.

Cursing, Daniel dropped Patrick to the floor and tried to find a way between the shrieking women. They were a mass of hair and claws that he wasn't sure how to penetrate. Lillian gave Kathryn's hair a good yank, putting a little space between them and giving Daniel an opening. Grabbing one in each hand, he ripped the girls apart. He wrapped Kathryn up under his arm, forcing her to bend over as he tossed Lillian back into a group of girls. "Get her out of here," he ordered.

The maidens wrapped hands around Lillian's arms, pulling her back before she could regain her balance and get to Kathryn, who was still struggling under Daniel's arm.

"Patrick can deal with you both tomorrow." He turned and forced Kathryn into her room, leaving Lillian in the capable hands of the other women. Kathryn stumbled as he released her and pushed her farther into the room. "Cool your head, girl," Daniel snapped as he went back out to collect Patrick.

The man sat, leaning against the wall, oblivious.

Pulling an arm over his shoulder, Daniel yanked the unconscious man to his feet and dragged him into Kathryn's room. Dumping him onto the bed, he growled, "If you care about this man at all, tend him," and stormed out. He was usually a patient man, but he'd had enough idiocy for one night.

Smoothing her hands over her rumpled hair, Kathryn watched Daniel leave. She turned to look at Patrick, sprawled on her bed. What had she gotten herself into? A knock on the open door drew her attention.

"Need help?" Bethany asked. A few of the other maidens stood there waiting.

Kathryn smiled at them. "Please." Maybe this wouldn't be such a long night after all.

Chapter Eight

PATRICK GROANED AS CONSCIOUSNESS FOUND HIM again. He felt horrible. Maybe losing one's self in a bottle of mead hadn't been the best idea he'd ever had. Rolling over, he stuck his face into the pillow, trying to block out the light filtering in. He drew in a deep breath, trying to clear his head. Something wonderful filled his nose. Patrick knew that scent. Pulling in a second lungful, he tried to identify the tantalizing smell. It tickled his back brain and made his dragon part curl in contentment. Whatever it was, he wanted to wake up to it more often.

Movement in the room drew Patrick's attention. He cracked an eye to see what was there but quickly shut it when light stabbed into his head, making it pound. This was not his room. Patrick stilled as he tried to figure out where he was. He tracked the sound of material rustling across the room.

"Good morning, My Lord."

Patrick's heart skipped at the sound of Kathryn's

sweet voice.

"I have your breakfast."

The bedding shifted as she sat on the edge of the bed and reached for him. Her fingers slipped into his hair, pushing it up away from his face. Now he knew what that alluring scent was. This wasn't his room or bed—this was hers. He turned his head slightly into her touch. It was heavenly. An angel's palm, sent to soothe his pains away.

Snaking an arm out, he caught her around the waist and pulled her to the bed. Kathryn squeaked in surprise as he rolled her in his arms. She struggled to get free, but the arms he'd wrapped her in pinned her back to his front. Growling, he buried his nose into the hair at the back of her neck.

Seeing she wasn't about to break his hold, Kathryn stopped struggling.

Patrick drew in a deep, contented sigh.

"My Lord?" Kathryn asked as she felt him relax behind her. The air from his breath tickled on the back of her neck.

"I'm sorry," he said, nuzzling deeper into her hair. "I'm not sure what I did, but I am sorry."

Kathryn relaxed in his hold. "No, My Lord." She sighed. "I'm the one who should be sorry. I didn't hear you out, and for that I apologize." She shifted around in his arms so she was looking into his eyes.

"I didn't mean to cause you so much grief."

Patrick studied her beautiful face. It was a sight he could get used to seeing in the morning.

"Master Daniel set me straight."

He let out a short snort of amusement. "What did Daniel say?" His voice was rough with sleep.

"That you're not a prince."

A sigh slipped from him as a hint of a smile curled his lips. He shifted in the bed, stretching a little. "No, I am no prince."

"He said you were an orphan."

The smile turned slightly ironic. "My parents were killed when I was just a babe," Patrick explained. "I was given into the care of the queen, but that does not make me anything. What else did Daniel tell you?"

Kathryn shifted in his arms, a little uncomfortable that he held her so close. "Just that you have a complicated life."

He searched her eyes, looking for something. "Yes," Patrick nodded slightly, "I do have a complicated life. I care about you greatly, but there are things you need to know about me. No matter how much I want you, I have to proceed with caution in matters of the heart." He paused, still searching her eyes for a reaction.

Kathryn waited patiently for him to finish.

Patrick's lips went thick with indecision. He wanted to tell her, but he was afraid she would have the same reaction she did when he'd told her he was the king's adopted son. "I want to tell you something," he said tentatively. "It's something that could hurt me greatly if it got out. Can I trust you to keep my secret?"

Kathryn tensed in his arms again. *This was it.* If she didn't promise, he would let her go, and they would be done. If she did agree, then she would be sworn to keep his secret, no matter how bad it was.

He waited as she weighed her options.

Slowly, she nodded. Her heart told her he was a good man and she could trust him.

Closing his eyes, he let out the breath he'd been holding. "I just have one thing to ask of you." Patrick opened his eyes and pinned her with them. "Give me the chance to explain this time."

Kathryn smiled at him. "Of course." She had been a fool to jump to conclusions before. She would hear all he had to say this time.

"Kathryn, I am a—"

Pounding on the door stopped his words.

"Lord Mylan?"

A male voice made them both freeze.

"*Yes?*" Patrick yelled back. His voice held a note of anger in it.

"The dragon is back!"

"I'll be right there," he called back and looked into Kathryn's eyes again. "I promise to finish this later." Leaning in, he kissed her quickly on the lips before releasing her and sitting up.

Kathryn rolled over and stood up from the bed, straightening her dress. She needed something to distract her from the feelings bubbling through her. That quick kiss had done odd things to her. Like having a swarm of butterflies set loose in her stomach. It scared her a touch.

"I brought you breakfast, My Lord." She busied her hands as he pulled himself from the bed. He was mostly dressed except for his boots and belt.

"No time," he grumbled as he tried to shove his foot into the wrong boot.

Kathryn snickered when he discovered his error and switched feet. "At least drink this." She held out a cup to Patrick.

Taking it up, he swallowed a large gulp from it and coughed, nearly spitting the dark liquid out. "What *is* that?" He looked into the cup. "It tastes like dragon dung."

Kathryn looked at him with concern. "Master

Daniel said it would help with your head. *What had Daniel put in that cup?*

Patrick looked up at her. "He did, did he?"

She nodded.

"Could be anything, then." Sighing deeply, Patrick drained the rest of the cup with a shudder. "Thank you." He gave the cup back to her waiting hands and went for his other boot.

Kathryn cradled the cup as she watched Patrick dress and leave. She was almost glad the dragon had come to interrupt them. The possibilities of what Patrick had wanted to say terrified her, but she would do as he asked. She would listen.

Setting the cup on the tray next to his untouched breakfast, she glanced back at the door. Patrick looked a shambles this morning. His rumpled shirt and cowlicked hair made her want to take him in her arms and hold him until he felt better. A hard night of drinking never did a man good. Hopefully, he was well enough to face off with the dragon today.

Patrick looked up at the black dragon. Another sack of gold rested by its leg. "The maidens aren't for sale." Sighing, he pushed his wet hair back out of his face. A rain barrel had provided a convenient place to stick his head before coming out to face the dragon.

The creature just snorted at him.

"You don't want these maidens, anyway," Patrick grumbled.

The dragon cocked his head curiously.

"They're flighty, they're finicky, and they make my life miserable."

What could have been amusement flashed across the dragon's eyes.

"There is only one among them I would consider worth it, and I hope someday she'll tend my brood."

This was met with a gurgle of sympathy from the large beast.

Patrick stopped and stared at the dragon as the epiphany struck him. "Eggs," he whispered. "That's why you need the maidens. You have eggs," he called a little louder.

A deafening roar shook the castle as the dragon shot a ball of fire at Patrick. The great beast took wing before the attack could hit.

Diving out of the way, Patrick barely avoided the sizzling flames. He sprawled on the ground, steaming. It was a good thing he had dunked himself before coming out. Pushing both hands through his hair, he worked through his thought.

"Patrick!" Daniel yelled as he came pounding up to check on the downed man. "What did you say to him?"

Bewildered at the possibilities, Patrick looked up from the ground. "When did the dragon first show up?"

Daniel stared at him, puzzled. "About eight weeks ago."

"And when did the dragon take the first of the girls?"

It took Daniel a moment to work out the math. "It's been a little over a fortnight. Why?"

"Do you remember how long it takes to hatch eggs?" Patrick asked as he pushed up from the ground.

Concern crossed Daniel's face. "Patrick?"

"Who's the fastest we have in wings?"

"Zane," Daniel answered without thinking. "Why?" He trailed Patrick as the lord practically ran back to the castle.

Patrick grabbed the closest guard. "Find me Zane. Now!" He sent the guard off running.

Daniel grabbed his friend's arm, stopping in him the courtyard. "Talk to me, Patrick."

A quick turn had him facing the man restraining him. "Suppose this dragon wasn't eating the maidens," Patrick posed.

"Okay."

"Why would a dragon need women?"

Daniel just shook his head. "There was no telling what a dragon would need maidens for."

"Eggs!" Patrick said the word like it was the answer to everything and turned back towards the castle, leaving Daniel standing there, shocked at the insane idea.

"Wait!" Daniel raced to catch up to Patrick. He fell into step with the frantic lord. "Explain."

"What do you know about hatching eggs?"

"Nothing," Daniel answered. "That's women's work."

"Exactly," Patrick pointed out. "If I'm right, the dragon needs someone to tend his eggs."

"But, why would he want maidens?"

"Who do you think takes care of the children when mothers are busy?"

"Why not take the mothers?"

Patrick stopped at the bottom of the castle steps and looked at Daniel, shocked. "Would *you* take a mother away from her child?"

"Of course not!" Daniel said, offended.

"Just because he's forgotten what he is doesn't mean he's a monster," Patrick pointed out. Looking up the steps, he found Kathryn and a few of the other maidens watching them. He swallowed before turning his attention back to Daniel. "If my hunch is right, he didn't eat the maidens." The gasp from the girls was audible. "Find me this dragon before his eggs hatch." He turned to go. "And send me Zane." He looked up longingly at Kathryn as he mounted the steps. Their conversation was going to have to wait until later. "I have a letter to write."

"I don't think this is a good idea," Daniel protested as Patrick gave Zane instructions.

Turning, Patrick faced the concerned man. "And what would you have of me?"

"We don't even know if he *has* eggs," Daniel retorted.

Patrick threw his hands out in exasperation. "Then explain his reaction. For heaven's sake, he threw a fireball at me."

"What did you say to him?"

"I asked him if he had eggs."

"I still don't see how the dragon stealing maidens means the creature has eggs. Are you sure you didn't hit your head when you fell?" Daniel asked.

Patrick glared at his friend. "The fall wasn't that bad." Letting out a forlorn sigh, Patrick dropped himself into the chair by his table. "It's the only thing that makes sense."

Zane watched quietly as the two men debated.

"Patrick, he wouldn't need to steal someone to

take care of his clutch. His mate would do it."

Patrick paused as he thought about that. "What if his mate couldn't? What if his mate was hurt or, God forbid, dead? Oh, God!" He looked up at Daniel, horrified. "He's lost his mate."

"You don't know that," Daniel said, trying to calm his friend.

Pushing up from his chair, Patrick paced as his thoughts churned. "But that's the perfect answer. Why else would a dragon that has never been an issue go rogue? He started with livestock. Food for his breeding mate. He killed the men of the castle after they banded together to hunt him down. He killed the rest when they came for his family. Maybe the lord's son actually found his clutch and hurt his mate. He only started taking the girls after the son's attack."

Daniel watched Patrick pivot and pace back across the room. "So why take more than one?"

The concerned man turned that thought over in his head as his feet worried the floor. "What if…" Patrick made another turn of the floor. "What if he's looking for someone who can take care of the eggs?"

"Then none of the maidens he's taken are going to do him any good. Why hasn't he asked us for help?" Daniel asked quietly.

Patrick stopped and stared at him. Obviously, Daniel hadn't stopped to think about that question.

The answer was so obvious. "Would you ask a castle full of strange men to help with your clutch?" The tone in his voice was almost sarcastic.

Daniel's eyebrows went up in surprise. He paused for a moment as he thought before turning to Zane. "Go." He waved the waiting man off. "Take the letter to the prince. Use what stealth you can, but this cannot wait until dark."

Zane bowed himself out.

Daniel looked back at Patrick. "We're basing this on a whole lot of 'ifs'. I hope you're right."

"Do you have other suggestions?" Patrick asked, hoping.

Letting out a long sigh, Daniel slowly shook his head. "No."

"Then I want every spare body out looking for that lair." Patrick turned to head towards the door. "We need to find him before something really bad happens."

A light tap on the open door drew Patrick's attention away from the map he was studying. Framed by the wood was a beautiful sight. Warmth spread through him at seeing the woman plaguing his heart. "Kathryn."

She smiled at him and stepped into his room.

Standing up, he went to her and took her hand. Her small hand fit into his perfectly as he caressed it. "I'm sorry I haven't gotten back to you."

A blush ran over Kathryn's cheeks, and she turned her face down. "It's all right, My Lord. You've been busy."

Letting out a forlorned sigh, he looked down at their joined hands. "That I have." He rubbed her soft skin again. Patrick loved the feel of it under his fingers. "But, I would like to finish our conversation from earlier."

"I would like that, too; but first, I need you."

Patrick raised a surprised eyebrow at her.

The color on Kathryn's cheeks deepened in embarrassment. "What I mean is, I need your help."

He smiled at her. "What can I do for you, my fair maiden?"

Kathryn raised her face to meet his eyes. "Nana needs some more herbs for her hands." The color started to fade from her skin as she spoke. "I asked Master Daniel if he could find someone to go with me to pick them, but he didn't have anyone to spare. He suggested that I come ask you."

"Gladly," Patrick said, raising her hand up to kiss it before releasing her. "Where would you like to go?" Turning, he grabbed his leather doublet from where he'd tossed it over the edge of the table.

"There's a willow stand down near the lake."

"I'm not sure where it is," Patrick admitted as he pulled on his coat, "but if you can guide me to it, I'll be glad to take you." He held his arm out for Kathryn to take.

"Certainly." She wrapped her hand around his arm, and they started out towards the bailey. "So what did you want to tell me?"

Patrick drew in a deep breath before letting it out very slowly. "I think that's a conversation best had when we reach the lake." He looked around for signs of the other young maidens. It was nice that they were being kind to him today, but he really didn't want them overhearing his confession. It could cause major issues. As it was, he was already taking a huge risk telling Kathryn, but he couldn't give in to his feelings until she knew the truth.

"As you wish," Kathryn answered. They walked on in silence, both preparing for the conversation that would take place once they reached the lake.

"My Lord."

Patrick turned to look at the man coming across the bailey with his horse. Apparently, Daniel had already anticipated this trip. "Thank you." He took the reins the man held out and released Kathryn. It took only a moment for Patrick to swing up into the saddle. "Shall we?" He held his hand down to the maiden.

She looked at the empty place at his waist. "Shouldn't you have a sword?" Reaching out, she took Patrick's hand and let him pull her up to the creature's back.

"Maybe." He didn't really need it. It wouldn't do him any good against the rogue dragon, and he was much more dangerous than any bandit they might meet, but if it made her happy...

Patrick looked around for the man who had brought him his horse. "My sword."

The man nodded and loped off to gather the missing weapon. It took him a few minutes, but he quickly came back and handed it up to the waiting pair.

Patrick took the leather scabbard. "Thank you." He tied it to the strap on the side of the saddle where he could draw it out if needed. "Are we ready now?" he asked Kathryn with a grin.

She smiled shyly and nodded.

Turning his attention back to the man, Patrick nodded. "We'll be back shortly." Holding Kathryn tightly in front of him, he pulled on the reins, wheeling the horse around. A swift tap with his heels set the animal into a smooth trot. "So where are we going, My Lady?" Patrick held her steady as the horse moved. He could easily get used to the feel of her against him.

Kathryn leaned back into the warm embrace. He felt so good pressed into her back. How could she ever have thought him self-centered and arrogant? She would enjoy just staying in his arms forever. Surprised by the directions her thoughts had gone, Kathryn sat up slightly so she wasn't pressed into him so hard. When had she stopped hating him?

"My Lady?"

Patrick's voice pulled Kathryn from her thoughts. "Yes?" she asked.

"Where are we going?"

She could hear the grin in his voice. It made her blush again. "That way." Kathryn pointed off to the right, in the direction of the huge lake just past the town. "It's a fair walk down the shore of the lake."

"Then we shall get there in no time," Patrick said before kicking his horse into a faster run. They cantered through the town and towards the lake.

The horse's ground-eating pace soon had the stand of aged willows in sight. "There." Kathryn pointed to the trees.

Patrick eased up on the horse and let the creature slow to a restful walk as they drew near. "Here?" he asked.

"Yes." Kathryn looked over the trees. Four willows stood clumped together in a neat circle.

Pulling the horse to a stop, Patrick carefully lowered Kathryn to the ground. Dismounting, he pulled the bit from the animal's mouth so it could graze on the soft, green grass. "Shall we?" He held his hand out, encouraging Kathryn to lead the way.

With a deep breath, Kathryn turned towards the grove. Picking a healthy-looking tree, she carefully pulled the shaggy bark off in strips, making sure not to take too much, lest she hurt the tree. She could feel Patrick's gaze on her. "So what did you want to tell me?" she asked. Maybe if she could get him talking, this would go a little easier.

Kathryn glanced up at him as she worked. There was a tension there that he normally didn't have. *Was he nervous?* Patrick drew in a deep breath, and the tension eased from him as he let it out. She could see he was committing himself to whatever decision he made.

"Even though it's only been a short time, I find I care greatly for you." His words were softly spoken as he walked towards her and the trees. He pushed his leather jacket off his shoulders as he moved. "But there are things that you should know about me."

Folding it up, he laid the coat on the ground next to her tree.

Kathryn focused on keeping her breathing steady as she watched Patrick pull off his leather belt. *Was he getting naked?*

Patrick rolled his belt up and dropped it on top of his coat. "I am not a normal man." He caught the heel of one boot with the toe of the other and pulled it loose.

Kathryn's breath caught as he took off his shoes. Oh yes, he was most definitely getting naked, but what should she do about it? "What do you mean?" she asked, trying to keep her eyes on her task and not on the slowly stripping lord.

"You already know that I was raised by the queen." Patrick crossed his arms over his loose shirt as he spoke. "Do you remember when I said that not all dragons were bad?"

Kathryn turned and looked at her lord, considering him. The only articles of clothing he had left were his shirt and pants, but she had a feeling those would be coming off soon, too. "Yes," she answered carefully. She had an uneasy feeling that her earlier thought about Patrick and dragons was turning out to be correct.

"Well." Slowly, Patrick came over, took the willow bark from her hands, and set it on the ground.

He pulled on her hands until she stood in front of him. The look in his eyes was intense as he said, "I'm a dr—"

The splashing of water and a roar was the only warning Patrick had. Grabbing Kathryn in his arms, he slammed them both to the ground and shifted to his grand form on top of her. His wings burst out in a fray of ruined material, and he cupped them around her as the first licks of dragon fire grazed across his back. He held her tightly, protected under his fire-proof scales.

When the raging inferno behind him ceased, he sprang off the terrified woman. Careful not to catch her under his sharp talons, Patrick turned to face the black dragon dripping in lake water. His tail thrashed back and forth in anger. "*Mine!*" Patrick hissed in dragon with his head dropped down and wings held wide, protecting Kathryn.

"*Maiden!*" the black dragon roared. Its chest bulged as it drew in a breath, stoking its fire for another attack.

Screaming in rage, Patrick launched himself at the creature three times his size. His teeth crunched into the hard scales on the bone frill, and he used his weight to yank the dragon's head back just as it opened its mouth. A great blast of fire fountained into the air, raining sparks down over the two dragons.

Kathryn watched in horror as the pair thrashed about. Part of her had expected Patrick to be a dragon. Taking off the restrictive pieces of his wardrobe led her to believe he would shift for her, but to have him do it on top of her was something else entirely. Her skin tingled from the magic and heat that had washed through him. Her gaze dropped from the dragons locked together to the singed scraps of material scattered across her. He had just saved her life. A great roar drew her bewildered mind back to the epic battle mere feet from her.

The black dragon shook furiously, trying to dislodge Patrick from the back of its head.

Ignoring the burn in his clenched jaw, Patrick sunk his talons as deep as he could get them into the black dragon's neck and held on for dear life. If the dragon should shake him loose, it would leave Kathryn unprotected. His eyes glanced over to her. She had managed to sit up, but she hadn't come to her senses enough to run off as his horse had. Patrick bit harder, making the rogue scream out in pain.

Furious, the black dragon tucked its wings in and rolled onto its back, crushing Patrick's wings down. The thing raised its long neck and slammed its head back into the ground, trying to break the painful hold Patrick had on its boned frill.

The jarring impact rattled the lord's brains around, but he held on as the dragon repeated the punishing slam. On the fourth impact with the ground, Patrick let go and scurried out from under the creature. The thing bashed its own head into the ground a fifth time. Hurrying over, Patrick placed himself between the attacking dragon and Kathryn. She still hadn't gotten herself together enough to run. "*Mine!*" he shrieked again as he lowered his head and thrashed his tail. He tucked his wings up against his body, easing the pain of being crunched under such a great weight. Thankfully, nothing seemed to be broken.

The black dragon rolled up onto its feet and retreated a few steps, gathering itself together. "Maiden!" it growled as it turned towards the pair.

"You cannot have my maiden!" Patrick yelled back. He no longer cared if the dragon had eggs

140

or not; no one attacked what was his and got away with it. His tail thumped into something solid, and he froze, afraid he might have hurt the woman behind him accidently. The soft feel of her hand on the fringy end of his tail distracted him from the danger in front of him, and he closed his eyes, trying to push the wave of pleasure back. Her fingers had run across a rather sensitive section.

Seeing Patrick's moment of inattention, the black dragon pounced, wrapping its jaws around his exposed neck. It yanked the smaller dragon up and shook him savagely, slamming him into the ground again.

"Patrick!" Kathryn cried out as she watched the creature drop the lord's limp body to the ground.

The rogue grabbed the lord by a wing and, with a great twist of its head, tossed the still lord far out into the lake.

"*No!*" Kathryn shrieked as Patrick hit the lake with a heart-breaking slap and slipped below the surface. Tears streamed down her face as she raced towards the water's edge. She could just see the tips of his red wings disappearing into the darkness. With a sick heart, she fell to her knees and watched her lord die, unable to do a thing about it.

The roar of the triumphant dragon shook her out of her grief. She turned just in time for the enormous creature to snatch her up. Its large wings sent out a great blast of air as the beast beat them down and launched into the air. Hope died in Kathryn's heart as her eyes skimmed across the still surface of the lake. Her lord was dead, and she would soon be the next victim of his murderer.

Chapter Nine

COLD SHOCKED PATRICK BACK INTO CONSCIOUSNESS. He tried to draw in a deep breath but got a lungful of water instead. Coughing, he snapped his eyes open to find he was sinking. Floundering, he righted himself and pushed to the surface of the lake. He drew in a great breath as soon as his head found air. Bobbing in the water, he worked to clear his mind as the cool liquid soothed the burning sensation in one of his wings. How did he get in the water?

Mine!

The memory hit him, and he scanned the shoreline, looking for signs of his maiden. She was not there. A distant roar drew his attention, and he twisted around to see the black dragon disappearing over the lake.

Mine!

Patrick kicked hard, trying to launch himself into the air to give chase, but the burn in his wing screamed and kept him from flapping it. He splashed back into the water, helpless. The wing was definitely dislocated, if not broken.

Tucking the injured limb up, Patrick lashed his tail and swam as fast as he could after the creature he was sure had stolen his maiden. If he was lucky, she was still alive. He turned his thoughts away from her possible death and concentrated on cutting through the water. Thankfully, that was one thing he was very good at. He could swim almost as fast as he could fly.

He had almost caught up to the black dragon when the creature did something that made his heart drop. It tucked its wings in and plummeted into the lake near the base of a rocky cliff. Patrick dove down and followed the great beast with his eyes.

The dragon lashed its tail back and forth, driving itself towards a dark place in the rock wall.

Patrick slowed his pace as the dragon slipped into the underwater cave. *So that's where the thing has been hiding.* It made sense now. The forest that Patrick's men had been losing the dragon in bordered this lake. The creature had probably been going in there, shifting to a lesser form, and losing its followers in the water. Few dragons actually swam, preferring the whip of the wind to the slush of waves. He didn't think any of his men would have suspected a wild dragon to take to the water.

Pausing, Patrick debated his choices. He could

go in there and confront the dragon, or he could go for aid. Every ounce of his instinct pushed him to rush in and reclaim what the beast had taken. *Mine!* But the ache in his wing reminded him he was already injured. There was no telling what other dangers he would have to face in the small cave. Snorting with displeasure, Patrick twisted in the water and whipped his tail, gaining speed. He wanted to fight his own battles, but he wasn't too proud or stupid to admit when he needed help. Going up against something as large as the rogue dragon with an injured wing was just suicidal.

As the far shore drew near, Patrick burst from the water and tried to take flight. With his horse gone, he had no time to spare in getting to the castle. A quick flight around the village would limit the contact the people would have with him. Pain ripped through his shoulder as he spread his wing. There was no way that thing would support him through the needed flight. Tucking it back up, he pulled himself from the water and stood, panting, while the spots cleared from his vision. There was no other choice, he needed to get his men and go after the dragon before it killed Kathryn. *Mine!*

Deciding to throw caution to the wind, Patrick bunched up his muscles and raced up the shoreline straight towards the town. There was no way around it. He couldn't get into the castle without going past the village. Maybe if he had been smaller in either of his forms, he could have snuck in, but he wasn't. The idea of shifting and running naked back to the castle crossed his mind, but he really didn't want to lose his dignity in front of the villagers. He was supposed to be their lord, and lords didn't do those types of things. Besides, he was nowhere near as fast in human form, and time was of the essence here.

Patrick pinned his eyes on the rising towers of the castle, visible through the rolling land. In just a moment, the town would be in sight, and he would have no choice but to follow the course he had chosen. His feet found a little extra speed as he committed to the action. If the people of the town came to run him out, so be it. He would do everything he could to save the woman he loved. *Mine!*

Screams rang out as Patrick raced his way through the village. He carefully dodged through the people moving about.

"*To arms!*" he roared as he passed the guards Daniel had sent to the village. The cry was picked up by human voices and echoed out, cutting through the screams of terror. The soldiers left their posts and followed their lord. For a moment, Patrick thought about how this looked to the villagers. A red dragon had just raced into their town, roared to draw the guards' attention, and raced out with a swarm of fighters on his heels. If nothing else, the villagers would think the men were giving it their all to protect them. Patrick smiled for a moment before sobering and putting an extra bit of speed into his run.

Cries of 'dragon' echoed through the bailey as Patrick skidded to a halt near the center of the enclosed space.

"*To wings!*" Patrick roared, turning in place as he looked for one person. He found him and raced towards the steps where Daniel was coming out of the castle. "Get the horns! Call the men back as fast as possible!" he cried, nearly bowling the man over.

"Patrick!" Daniel's hands caught the frantic lord's injured wing. "Calm down!"

Patrick roared in pain and dropped himself to the ground to keep from accidently lashing out and hurting someone.

Daniel stood there in shock, looking at the downed lord. What in the world would drive Patrick to throw away everything they had been working for and show himself as dragon? He shook free of his surprise and glanced around at the chaos in the bailey. "Speak!" he ordered.

"He has Kathryn," Patrick growled from where he remained on the ground. "I know where he took her."

Surprise and understanding passed through Daniel. The kidnapping of one's potential mate would definitely drive a dragon to rash actions. He grabbed one of the men rushing past and pulled him to a stop. Patrick had already blown their cover with the townspeople, and if the lord knew where the dragon was, it was time to act. They would deal with the consequences later. "Take the horns to the towers and call the men back. Four short blasts and two long."

The man's eyes widened at the signal, but he nodded and rushed to carry out the order. The signal would ring throughout the land, calling the scouts back as quickly as possible. They would come en masse, on wing.

"Explain," Daniel demanded as he reached out and touched Patrick's wing. It hung at an odd angle. He shifted it around to see how badly damaged it was. Thankfully, it looked to just be out of socket.

"We were out at the lake," Patrick growled. "The dragon attacked from the water. I couldn't stop it." There was a pained note in his voice that had nothing to do with his physical injury.

"And where did it go?" Daniel asked. He braced

himself on Patrick's shoulder and wrapped his hands firmly around the long bone of Patrick's wing.

"An underwater cave," Patrick explained as he forced himself to relax under his friend's firm grip.

That explained why they couldn't find the lair. Daniel drew in a calming breath as he yanked the dislocated bone back into place, driving a roar from the lord. A scream sounded from the doorway, drawing their attention. A group of maidens peeked out at the red dragon Daniel was helping.

"You have just made our lives here *very* hard," Daniel reprimanded his lord as he released the wing.

Patrick let out a puff of smoke. "I know," he grumbled as he worked his way up from the ground. Tucking his wings in, he sat down and wrapped his tail around his feet. "I have made my choice, and I will live with it."

Daniel gave him a hard look. *Did the lord not realize he had just jeopardized all of his men, too?*

"The dragon's lair is not a place we will be able to get to in human form," Patrick explained. "I fear for the girls he had dragged into that watery hell."

"Then we will do as we must." Daniel turned away from his lord to look at the men waiting for orders. A horn cried out the signal from the top of the tower. He paused for a moment to look up at the maidens gathering in the doorway. They had grown

149

bold and were stepping from the safety of the castle to look at the red dragon glistening in the sunlight.

Daniel glanced at his lord. Patrick really did make a striking sight. But the ladies were in for a whole lot more in just a moment. Daniel turned from them and looked out over the men. "*To wings!*" he bellowed.

The call echoed through the men, and they started to strip out of their clothing and shift to their grand dragon forms. The girls gasped as a sea of dragons erupted in front of them. Greens and blues made up the majority of the mass with an occasional red. Only one black body broke the display of flashing scales. Daniel smiled at his men, slipping into their ranks. *Oh yes, now that was truly a sight to behold!*

Daniel slipped through the throng of dragons, barking orders. A few would remain here to protect the women as the rest went out to face their foe. Once the orders were given, Daniel passed Patrick and headed up the steps to where the maidens and Nana stood. The girls were terrified, but the older woman just smiled at him.

"I knew what you were," Nana said as she beamed at the younger-looking man. "I was very young when the purge happened, but I still remember the musk of dragons."

Crafty old woman! Daniel smiled at her. "Thank

you for trusting us." He held her hand and bowed over it.

She patted his cheek lovingly. "You have been so good to us. It's nice to know your kind still survives."

Daniel's grin spread as he stood up. "We were never gone." Releasing her hand, he started to pull off his clothing as well. The pleasure dropped away from him as he pulled off his shirt. He looked over the confused girls huddled behind Nana. "Part of the men will remain here to protect you in case the dragon gets past us, but fear not. They will see you come to no harm."

Patrick let out a reaffirming growl that caused the women to bunch up in fright.

Daniel just shook his head and came back down the steps. He placed Patrick between himself and the woman and stripped down to shift into his grand form. He stretched his green wings out. *Lord, it felt good to be back in scales.* A quick scan of the men found that they had formed up in loose lines with the smallest in front. Daniel let out a snicker. Even in his grand form, Patrick was easily the smallest of all of them.

Turning back to the business at hand, he looked over at the lord. "Shall we wait for the scouts?" There were six holes in the ranks waiting to be filled.

Patrick shook his head. "No. The guards can

send them to find us at the lake." He cocked his head and gave Daniel a grin that looked a lot scarier than it should have. "I don't think they could miss a full flight of dragons."

Daniel rumbled with laughter. "Then let us be off." He looked down at his lord. "Will you be able to fly?" He was worried about the man stressing his injured wing so soon after having it set.

Patrick spread out his wings and pumped them a few times, but he didn't get off the ground. "No," he sighed. "But I will meet you at the water's edge near the stand of willow trees. After that, I should have no problems keeping up."

Daniel scoffed at him. "You may even beat us to the cave." The man could swim like no other dragon Daniel had ever seen.

Patrick laughed. "That I might."

Turning his attention to the men, Daniel sized them up. "To the lake!" he yelled. Wings beat the air into submission, lifting huge bodies off the ground.

Patrick sat quietly as the flight took to the skies and sailed out over the village. It was amazing to see so many dragons flying together. The majestic sight made his heart swell with pride. Now, if he could just get the townspeople to understand…

Turning away from his men, he looked up at the awed ladies. Patrick had watched the girls carefully as the men had shifted to dragon. There had been a strange mixture of fascination and fear on all of their faces. Only Nana smiled happily at them. *So the old woman had known what they were… but for how long? And if she had caught on, how many others in the village knew?* Something else he had to think about before confronting the town with their existence. Maybe his decision wouldn't end with them being run out of the castle by angry mobs.

Standing up, he ruffled his wings and tucked them back along his body. It was time he got moving. As it was, he was already going to be well behind the faster flyers.

The lord's movement caught the ladies' eyes. They all stared at him. The look of fear had faded from their eyes.

Patrick dropped them a low bow, before turning and racing off through the open gates. A roar sounded from the guards as he passed under them. The sound was picked up by the flight and rattled the entire valley. If nothing else, this would be a day that all would remember for a very long time.

Patrick was tired by the time he reached the stand of willow trees. Plopping down in the cool grass, he stretched his aching muscles out, trying to ease the burn. He hadn't run that far in a long time.

"Nice of you to join us," Daniel teased as he came over to check on the lord.

Patrick glowered up at him. "Is everyone here?" he growled, stretching his wings out. The joint he had dislocated was still sore, but there was a possibility it would hold him in flight.

Daniel looked around at the dragons waiting. "You're the last." Anticipation was thick in the air as the men keyed themselves up for the coming battle.

Now all Patrick had to do was lead the men to the underwater cave. "Good." Pushing himself up from the ground, he flapped a few times, debating if he would fly or swim. He could lead them better if he flew, but that cool water would feel wonderful on his heated skin. He looked over at his second. "Can you follow me if I swim?"

Daniel cocked his head, the dragon version of a raised eyebrow, and considered him. "How deep are you going to be?"

"Not very."

"Then we can follow you."

Drawing in a deep breath, Patrick nodded.

"Then assemble the men." He wanted to get this over with as quickly as possible. Just the thought of what that black dragon was doing to his fair maiden ate away at him. *Mine!*

Barking orders, Daniel soon had the dragons lined up and ready for action.

"Listen!" Patrick's voice cut across the group's rumbling, pulling them to silence. "The entrance to the rogue's lair is an underwater cavern set in the rock cliffs on the other side of the lake." He stood up and paced the line as he briefed the fighters. "It's about twenty feet down and just larger than the dragon himself." Pausing to let this sink in, he turned and paced back down the line. "I did not go inside, so I do not know what we will find there. I suspect that the rogue has a clutch of and the stolen maidens—"

Shock sounded through the ranks.

Patrick paused in his briefing to wait for the sound to die down. He gave them all a pointed look. "It would probably be best to draw him out before engaging him. I want this dragon *alive*, so do your best to restrain him. But if all else fails, take him down."

A murmur of understanding sounded through the men.

"Then let's go!" Patrick turned and led the way to the lake as the rest of the flight took to the air.

Daniel led the group out over the lake as Patrick

slipped into the water. They would win this day even if he had to take the dragon down himself. *Mine!* had to be saved.

Chapter Ten

IT TOOK HIM A MOMENT TO GET INTO WATER DEEP
enough to swim, but Patrick had no problem
catching up to the flight and passing them. He stayed
close enough to the surface that wings threw out
great wakes as he passed. It would have been faster
to dive a little deeper and not break the surface of
the lake, but he didn't want to lose the flight in the
murky water.

Seeing the rock wall, it only took Patrick a moment to locate the entrance to the cave. He pushed
past the pain in his wing and shot out of the lake towards Daniel. "Here!" He flapped, hovering just over
the surface of the water.

Daniel let out a warbling cry, and a single blue
dragon folded his wings and splashed down into
the water. The long seconds ticked past as everyone
stared at the glassy surface of the lake.

Bobbing in the air, Patrick clenched his jaw
against the pain tearing through his wing. As it was,

he was not flapping it enough to stay stable. He was just considering dropping back into the water to ease the ache when the blue dragon burst from the water and flapped hard away from the surface. A great blast of fire raced after him, sizzling the water as it passed.

The black dragon erupted from the lake with a roar and attacked the first thing it could see through the rising steam. Unfortunately, it was the bright red scales of Patrick's hide.

The unexpected crunch of teeth sent shivers of pain through Patrick's already-injured wing. He didn't fight as the dragon shook him violently and dropped his limp form to the lake below. A roar of anger echoed in the men waiting, and the battle commenced above. Giving in to the throbbing in his wing, Patrick left the men to deal with the dragon. No matter how strong or enraged he was, there was no way the rogue could stand against more than a score of Elites.

Turning his attention to the cave, Patrick tucked up his wings and swam into the opening. Just inside, the passage made a sharp turn up, and it took no time for the lord to break the surface of the water inside the cave. *So, this was where the creature had been hiding.* He cast his eyes around, taking in the scene.

A great cavern opened up with high ceilings. Light from some fire glistened against the distant stalactites. Carefully, Patrick pulled himself up to the edge of the sandy floor. His hunch was right. Along the back were six eggs, glistening in the low light. Another black dragon lay next to them.

This dragon watched him closely as he slinked close. It growled a warning.

Patrick dropped to the ground in as nonthreatening a way as he could. "My Lady," he called out to the dragon. From the way it curled protectively around the eggs, he was sure this was the mother of the brood. "I mean you no harm."

The dragon didn't move, but curiosity shone in her glistening eyes. "Speak your name," she called to him.

Patrick stood up and wrapped his tail around his feet in a dignified manner. Her ability to understand him and speak boded well. "I am Patrick Mylan."

"*Mylan!*" The dragon lifted her head as soon as she heard his name. Letting out a pain-filled groan, she dropped herself back to the sand.

"My Lady!" Patrick cried out and shifted back to his human form. He raced to her side. Even an idiot could see she was in serious pain.

"Forgive me, My Lord." The dragon turned one great eye to him. It was glassy with agony. The fact that she called him lord showed that she knew who he was, but that wasn't saying much. Most dragons knew of the orphaned red dragon the queen had taken in.

"Be still." There was definitely something wrong here. Patrick placed his hand on her side and felt her temperature. It was much too high, even for a dragon. "What happened?" he asked.

The dragon let out a shuddering breath and shifted her wing to show a bolt stuck in her side.

Patrick clenched his teeth. The bolt was from a crossbow—not something a farmer would have. "How?" he asked as he felt around the wound. It was obvious the bolt had been in there for some time now. The flesh around the entry had already started to sour. If they didn't get her help soon, she would die. As it was, it would take a skilled magician to ease the dragon's pain. This had gone far beyond the aid of a simple healer.

"From the castle." Her breath was labored as she spoke.

Patrick rubbed her side, soothing her as best he could. There was only one castle near here, and the black dragon had already razed its occupants. No wonder he had gone in and killed all the men. They had nearly killed his mate. "And the maidens?" Patrick asked, needing to know that Kathryn was all right.

"Safe," the dragon groaned.

Patrick's heart lightened at her words. "I promise that we will get you help." He patted the dragon's side again. Backing away from her, he shifted back into dragon form and raced to the water's edge. He paused long enough to reassure her again before diving into the water. There were three dragons in the flight that might have the skill to save the woman's life. Hopefully they weren't too late.

Patrick broke the surface of the water into hell.

His men had the black dragon surrounded and were taking turns attacking him, but no one was really doing damage. They were trying to draw him over land so they could down and capture him, but the rogue had other ideas.

He hovered over the water, just outside the cave. Anytime a dragon would go for the lake, the black dragon would attack viciously, driving them back up.

Seeing an opening, Patrick beat his wings hard and shot straight up at the beast. He wrapped his talons around his neck and put his mouth right next to his ear. "Stop this!" he screamed. "We are not your enemies!"

The loud noise rattled the dragon for a second. He shook his head, trying to ease the ringing and dislodge his attacker.

Patrick held firm. "Your lady is dying!" he shrieked again. Please let his words register in the dragon's mind. "Stop this, and we can save her!"

The entire flight of dragons stopped their attack.

The dragon let out a deafening roar and shook his head again, but the beating of his wings slowed, letting them slip into the water.

Patrick held on for a few more seconds before releasing his hold on the surrendering dragon. He turned his eyes skywards to the surrounding dragons, looking for the ones he wanted. "Mica! Andrew! Thalin!" he barked. "With me!"

Diving into the water, the three dragons followed as Patrick led them into the cave and up to the sandy floor.

"Save her." Patrick pointed towards the injured dragon.

The three men shifted and went to her. They all grimaced at the severity of the wound.

Andrew turned to Patrick with despair in his voice. "My Lord?"

The growl of the rogue dragon echoed around the room. The dark creature pulled himself from the water and lay down on the sand.

The man blanched. "We can't work magic without the right components," he explained.

"Maybe we can help."

Patrick's heart leaped to his throat. He knew that sweet voice. *Mine!*

Kathryn came around the back end of the injured dragon with the maidens that were missing. Each carried an armload of supplies. Pausing, Kathryn glanced at the red dragon before turning to the three men standing next to the wounded dragon. *Oh my god, they were naked!* Color climbed up her cheeks, but she pushed her embarrassment away and approached them with a bowl wrapped in a cloth. "Here." She set the bowl near the men and backed up a step. "Fever's foe."

The girls quickly dropped their armloads of herbs and bandages on the ground and hid behind Kathryn.

The three men bent to look at the supplies. One of the men looked up at the girls. "Is there more?"

"Yes," Kathryn answered. She pointed towards the back of the cavern. "There's a whole room filled with random things."

He stood up and started off towards the room. "Show me."

Two of the girls hurried off leading the way, leaving Kathryn to deal with the dragons.

Movement caught her eye, and she turned to look at the red dragon. The thing chirped and rumbled as it stepped closer.

The younger girls huddled behind Kathryn, scared of the growling, red beast.

Kathryn froze and studied the creature before her. It was nowhere near as large as the other dragons. A trickle of smoke curled up from one nostril as it let out a series of growls and clicks. Its scales were the color of bright blood. Several were marred from recent battle. One wing drooped lower than the other. Could this beast be her Patrick? But hadn't the black dragon killed him? Memories tickled the back of her mind as she stepped towards him. A flash of red scales in the early morning light. She had seen this dragon before.

"It was you." Kathryn pulled away from the girls trying to hold her back. "You jumped out of the lake that morning."

Sitting back on his haunches, the dragon curled his tail around his feet and nodded. He hung head hung in a shameful way, showing he was sorry that he has scared them. There was something about the way he moved that convinced her she was right. This was most definitely her Patrick.

Kathryn launched herself at him. Her arms

wrapped around his neck, and she squeezed him for all she was worth. She didn't care if he was a dragon—he was alive, and that was all that mattered. "I thought you were dead." She buried her face into the side of his neck as tears burned free. "I watched you sink in the lake."

Joy washed through Patrick as he lifted up his front leg and wrapped it around the crying girl. "It would take more than that to kill me," he purred. He held her for a moment, glad she was alive and not afraid of him. *Mine.*

A scream of pain from the female dragon broke into their world. The mages had started to work fever's foe into the wound. "My Lord!" Thalin called for help.

Patrick released Kathryn and rushed to the injured dragon's side. Their reunion would have to wait for a more appropriate time.

"Hold her down," Mica yelled as the dragon thrashed about.

Throwing himself on her neck, Patrick tried to pin her but failed. She easily outweighed him by more than three times his weight. He glanced back at her mate. He was big enough to hold her down. "If you want to save her, help me!" Patrick roared.

The black dragon shifted from foot to foot, distressed by his mate's pain.

Now Patrick understood why the dragon had been stealing woman. He needed someone to heal his mate, but he couldn't mentally handle her being hurt. Seeing the larger dragon's indecision, Patrick released his hold on the injured female. He raced over and rammed his head into the side of the larger dragon. "Hold her down." He banged his head into the black scales once more before the dragon moved. *Bloody dragon!*

Nipping at the great creature's scales, Patrick drove the reluctant beast to his mate. Laying his body over hers, the larger male pressed her down. "Not too hard!" Patrick snapped. The rogue lifted his weight so she was pinned but not squished. Patrick went back and draped himself over the injured dragon's neck.

Seeing that they held the dragon as best they could, Patrick nodded to the mages. "Go!" he cried.

The two men turned their attention back to their work.

The female dragon let out a roar of pain as they prodded the sore flesh.

Two more dragons, a green and a blue, climbed out of the water. "My Lord!" the green chirped.

Patrick looked over at them as he bounced

around on the dragon's thrashing neck. Help had arrived. *Finally!*

"The eggs!" he cried.

The new dragons looked at the clutch dangerously close to the side of the thrashing dragons.

"My Lord?" The blue dragon cocked his head, unsure what Patrick wanted.

Bloody male dragons!

Growling, Patrick jumped off the writhing dragon. "Hold her!" he snapped.

If you want something done right…

The dragons quickly came up and pinned the injured dragon's tail and neck.

Backing up, Patrick turned his attention to the fragile eggs. Two of them had already been knocked over. *Please let the babies be okay.* Carefully, he came over and nosed them. They were whole, but they wouldn't stay that way long if he left them there much longer. He couldn't do anything for the female, but he could make sure her young were safe. He had to get them away from the chaos. Pushing it with his nose, he rolled the first one across the sand until it was well away from the struggling dragon.

Patrick was surprised when he saw Kathryn grab the two terrified girls.

"Come on," she cried as she pulled them towards the eggs. Together, they laid a third and fourth egg over and rolled them across the sand.

Leave it to women to know what needed to be done! He could kiss them all. "Carefully," Patrick chirped at the women.

Taking each egg in turn, he arranged them together on the sand and fussed over their placement until he was happy. The eggs sat in two neat rows with a space between them. Finally, they were safe, but the sand here was much too cold for the young. It was time to get them back up to temperature. "Watch yourselves," Patrick rumbled as he slipped between the girls and the eggs. He drew in a few deep breaths, stoking his fire before letting a stream of white-hot flames out towards the eggs. The girls backed away from the heat as Patrick circled the clutch, warming them.

Patrick lowered the intensity of his flames as the sand started to melt. He needed to warm the eggs, not cook them. After two full circles, he slipped into the space between them and lay down. Spreading his wings out, he covered the eggs, holding in the heat radiating from the hot sand. God, he felt foolish incubating eggs, but the roll across the cold ground would not have been easy on the babies inside. It was best to get them back up to temperature quickly before any permanent harm was done.

Kathryn watched as Patrick tended the clutch. He made taking care of the dragon's young look easy. In the short time Kathryn had been in the cave, she had avoided going near the fragile-looking eggs. Their black shells looked like they were made of sparking glass. In truth, they were somewhat soft, like hard leather—their glossy surface gave the wrong impression. Hopefully, Patrick knew what he was doing and wouldn't cook the poor babies in their shells.

Turning back to the scene behind her, Kathryn tried to figure out what to do. It didn't appear that her help was needed anywhere. The missing man had come back with another armload of supplies and was busy preparing to take the bolt out of the thrashing dragon. The girls who had gone with the mage knelt near the men, ready to help if they could. The other maidens had settled to the sand a safe distance from the dragons to watch.

Kathryn looked around one more time before heading over and standing in front of Patrick's head. She could feel the heat radiating from him, but his wings held most of it in. The thought of sitting next to a dragon gave her a moment of pause, but the look of longing he gave her eased her fears. *This was Pat-*

169

rick. He may be a dragon, but he was the same man that she had come to care for.

After a moment of indecision, she braved the heat and folded herself down on the sand next to his head. It was a little warm, but not uncomfortably so. His head thumped softly into her side as he rolled it against her and let out a very contented sigh. Kathryn smiled and raised her arm up to rest over him. His scales were smooth and warm under her hands as she traced their patterns.

"You really are beautiful." Kathryn sighed as she shifted to watch the mages work. Her fingers played across his scales, driving a purr of contentment from him.

Another dragon climbed from the water. Patrick looked up at Daniel. Although the grin didn't show on his face, amusement twinkled in the dragon's eyes as he watched his lord sitting on eggs, nestled next to a maiden.

"Don't you even dare!" Patrick growled, shooting him a look that could kill.

Daniel feigned innocence. "I would never dream of it." His eyes followed the hand petting his lord's head.

Patrick glowered at him. There were going to be limericks about this tomorrow.

Turning towards the pile of dragons, Daniel took stock of the situation. The three mages worked to clear the bolt from the wound as the female dragon thrashed about in pain. "I see you were right."

The injured dragon screeched as the men ripped the barbed head from her side. One of her wings slipped out from under her mate and smacked the men by her side. Two of them fell backwards into the area where the delicate eggs had been.

Daniel chuckled as the men scrambled up and back to the gushing wound. He looked down at Patrick. "Good call." Daniel settled on the sand to watch the men pack and enchant the wound.

Patrick just snorted and rolled his head a little farther into Kathryn's side. Now they just had to wait.

Chapter Eleven

EVENTUALLY, THE CHAOS SETTLED DOWN. ONCE THE herbs and magic eased the female's pain and her life was no longer in danger, she curled up with her mate, exhausted. His contented purrs rumbled through the sand.

Patrick rested his head against Kathryn's side. He knew exactly how the rogue felt. The feel of Kathryn's fingers scratching over his scales had set him purring a while ago. His contentment was interrupted when Mica came over to check on the eggs. The mage cringed away from the heat as Patrick raised his wings to show off the precious hoard.

"You sure have them hot enough." The man braved the heat as he got closer to them. "Where did you learn to tend eggs?"

Patrick let out a resigned snort. If actually sitting on the eggs hadn't earned him new limericks, this surely would. "You know the queen is very hands-on with her subjects," he grumbled.

Mica nodded. He went to the other side to check on the second set of eggs.

"Well, she used to take me to the hatcheries when I was little." The queen had coaxed Patrick into helping heat and turn eggs.

"And I am sure she is glad you did." Mica nodded back to the resting dragon. "You have done a fine job here."

Patrick lowered his wings once more, trying to hold the heat in. Yeah, tending eggs was a fine skill he never thought he would actually need. Just went to prove that you never learn anything completely worthless.

"What did he say?" Kathryn asked.

Mica smiled broadly as he considered the girl. Mischief glinted in his eye. "He used to help the queen when she tended the hatcheries. I hear tell he was pretty good with eggs. The young maidens at court were always after him to sit on their clutches."

So the man knew more than he'd claimed! Patrick thumped his tail angrily on the ground. "Mica! I will eat you," he growled.

It was true, his status as orphan had left him free game to the dragon maidens of the court, and being the adopted son of the king had made him a prime subject for pretend father to many clutches of eggs. At least, until he realized he could tell them no and they couldn't do more than cry. But by that time, he had spent hours with rocks under his wings, pretending they were eggs.

Mica chuckled at the threat in the lord's words. "Let me see your wing." The mage stepped closer to inspect the injured joint.

Patrick hissed as the man applied pressure on the wound. *Damn that hurt!*

"Well, it doesn't appear broken." The man stepped back from the heat. "Looks like you might have dislocated it. Resetting it will have to wait until you're off those eggs."

Tell me something I don't know! Patrick nodded. "Then get someone in here to sit on these."

Daniel rumbled with laughter. "I'll see what I can do about finding a volunteer." Lifting himself from the sand, he turned back to the edge of the water, amused.

"Don't tell them what they're volunteering for." Patrick raised his head and yelled at his second. "If they know it's to sit on eggs, they'll run." They may be willing to take on a rogue dragon, but eggs scared most men.

Daniel rumbled again as he slipped into the water.

Patrick laid his head back down and rolled it so he could see Kathryn next to him. Contentment washed through him again. *Mine!* She looked okay, but the other girls had been here longer. Hopefully they were okay, too. Patrick turned his attention back to the mage. "Check out the maidens," he called to Mica.

Mica nodded. "Are you hurt, My Lady?" he asked Kathryn.

Kathryn looked at the dragon, then up to the nude man. She turned her face away from him, blushing her embarrassment. "I'm fine."

Patrick snorted out a soft laugh. Obviously, with all the excitement, she had forgotten the men were naked.

Mica bowed to them both and turned to check on the other ladies.

Patrick was glad when Daniel finally returned with two of the smaller dragons in the flight. He was starting to cramp up from lying still for too long.

Turning, Daniel looked at each of the new dragons. "Go lay next to Lord Mylan—one on each side—and be careful of the eggs."

The two dragons looked at each other. "Eggs?" one asked. "I thought you said we would be on guard duty." He looked over towards the two black dragons curled together.

"You are." Daniel grinned at them—a terrifying gesture on the face of a dragon. "You get to guard the eggs. Now, make sure they are safe and warm."

Patrick snickered at Daniel's deviousness. Trickery would be the only way to get the warriors to sit on eggs.

Reluctantly, the pair of volunteers came over and snuggled up next to the clutch.

Kathryn backed away as Patrick wiggled out from under the wings of his replacements. Turning around, he gave them a pointed glare. "Don't let them get cold," he warned. The queen would tan all of their hides if they let something happen to those babies. Now free from the eggs, Patrick held his wing out for Mica's healing hands.

With a quick jerk, the mage had Patrick's wing reset. "You may want to stay off that for a few days," he warned the lord.

That went without saying. Patrick nodded and looked around. Now that things had settled down, it was time for him to get out and send a message to the prince. They were going to need someone from the royal hatcheries to come help with the eggs. Once the pair sitting on the eggs got out and warned the others, they were going be hard pressed to find volunteers for anything.

Turning his mind away from the egg-sitting issue, Patrick considered the cave and its watery entrance. "Is there another way out?" he called to the men now milling around. It would be nice if they didn't have to swim out. The dragons could do it easily, but the women would have to be carried.

Mica turned and asked the question of the maidens.

"Not that we have found," the youngest of them answered.

"Then we will have to take them out by water," Patrick confirmed. Not a choice he really wanted to make, but they would manage it. He looked over at Mica. "Explain it to them," he growled.

It took a little while to convince the girls of the plan, but soon they were all matched up with a dragon that would carry them through the water and out of the cavern. All except one.

"But I want to go with *you*," Kathryn complained to Patrick as Mica tried to get her to pair up with him. There was no way she was going to make that trip again unless it was with Patrick.

"He can't take you," Mica insisted. "He has a hurt wing and cannot fly when he gets out of here."

"I don't care." Kathryn pressed herself into Patrick's side. "I've lost him once today, and I don't intend to let him go again." She wrapped her arm around his neck near his shoulder.

The purr Patrick let out rumbled up her side. Bending his neck around, he caught the edge of her skirt in his teeth. Kathryn followed as he pulled her around and rubbed his head into her middle. He chirped and squeaked something that she didn't understand. Warm air washed through her clothing as he drew in her scent.

Kathryn wrapped her arms around his head. "I'm not leaving you." She leaned forwards and placed a kiss on his head. No matter what he said, she would not allow someone else to take her out.

A snicker slipped out of him, and he nudged her with his nose.

Releasing her love, Kathryn backed up to look at him.

He chirped at her again, but she still didn't understand him. He turned and chirped at the waiting mage.

Mica nodded and looked up at Kathryn. "He says he will not leave you, but he can't carry you out of here."

"I will not go with anyone else," Kathryn said. Crossing her arms over her chest, she turned around, ignoring the men. She thought she had lost Patrick once already. She would not leave without him.

Patrick chirped again and rustled his wings.

"My Lord?"

The concern in Mica's voice caused Kathryn's ears to perk up. She listened as Patrick shifted in the sand and chirped again.

"But that will leave a hole in your armor," Mica warned.

The one side of the conversation Kathryn could understand disturbed her. She turned around to watch the men.

Patrick chirped again and shut his eyes.

Mica shrugged and ran his hand over Patrick hide. Horror raced through Kathryn as the man found a loose scale and slipped his nail under it. He was going to tear a piece out of Patrick's hide! "What are you doing?" Kathryn asked as saw Mica wiggling the scales back and forth. "Stop that!" She came over and tried to stop the mage, but he had already gotten the scale loose.

Patrick groaned as Mica ripped the scale off.

Kathryn gasped at the trickle of blood that ran out of the wound. Shoving the mage out of the way, she pressed the end of her skirt against the hole, trying to stop the bleeding. *Why would Patrick let the mage do such a thing to his beautiful hide?*

179

The hole where Mica had pulled out the scale ached, but it was Kathryn's concern that made the pain bearable. Patrick let out an amused chuckle as he shifted back to his human form.

Kathryn gasped in surprise.

Catching up her hand, he pulled her into his arms. God, she felt good against him.

Shock held her stiff in his embrace.

"It's all right," he whispered as he held her. "It will grow back." His hand ran down her back, soothing her. "Thank you for defending me." Pleasure tingled through him as he held her. *Mine.*

As she slowly relaxed against him, Kathryn wrapped her arms up around his shoulders, holding him to her. "I thought I lost you." Her voice wavered with remembered fears. Laying her head on Patrick's shoulder, Kathryn buried her face in the crook of his neck.

Patrick could feel her tears trickling down his chest. "Shhh," he soothed her, stroking his hand down her back again. Tilting his head over, he rested it on hers, comforting her as she cried. "It takes more than that to put me down." Not *much* more, but he did survive it. After a moment, he sighed. "But what

Mica said is true."

Kathryn raised her head to look at him.

"I could carry you out of here, but the swim across the lake would likely drown us both." He raised his hand up and caressed her face, wiping her tears away. "I promise I will never leave you." He gazed into her eyes, gauging her reaction as he spoke. "We have much to talk about, but dragons bond for life. I am yours, if you will have me."

Surprise, fear, and delight flashed across her face. She froze as answering words eluded her.

Patrick leaned in and kissed her before she could find something to say.

She melted in his arms again.

"You don't have to answer me now," he said as he held her, "but I do have something for you." Releasing her, he caught her hand before turning to Mica.

Kathryn's eyes fell to the flash of red as Patrick took the scale from the waiting mage. They followed it down as Patrick wiped the scale across his thigh, cleaning the blood away. Blushing, she turned her face away from him.

Letting out a soft laugh of amusement, Patrick held the scale up between them. "This is for you."

Kathryn turned back and looked as the crimson scale. It sparkled in the low light of the cavern. "What?" she asked as Patrick raised her hand and laid the glittering piece in her palm.

"It's customary to share a scale with one's chosen mate." He closed her fingers around the warm scale. "Usually, the process is more complicated than this, but a true sharing can wait for a more appropriate time." He took a deep breath and let it rush out of him as he looked down. "Something else we will need to talk about."

Waving the issue away for a more appropriate time, he looked back into her eyes. "For now, I want you to keep this." He wrapped his hand around hers, closing his scale inside her fist. "This is my promise to you. I will not leave you." Folding her arm up against her chest, he pulled her back into his arms so her hand was pinned between them. "I love you."

Joy flashed across Kathryn's face as she yanked her arm out from between them and threw it around Patrick's neck. "I love you, too." Tears burned in her eyes as she held him and smothered his face in kisses.

Laughing, Patrick caught her head in his hand, pressing his lips to hers. After a moment longer, he released her from the kiss. He held her to him, letting his emotions roll through him. He had held women before, but none of them stirred his soul the way a true-bonded mate could. They still had much to discuss, but he let himself embrace the instincts pulling him towards her. *Mine*. The thought had been passing through him all day, but this had a note of finality to it that warmed his heart. Even if she decided that life with a dragon was too much, he would always be hers.

Drawing in her scent one last time, Patrick nuzzled her hair before pushing her back out of his arms. He looked around at the cavern once more. Guards were set, both to watch the two rogue dragons and to keep the eggs warm. He would have to contact the prince as soon as they got back to the castle. Hopefully, Zane had already made it with his letter, and things would be in motion. His biggest problem would be dealing with the townspeople. *Oh, that was going to be a joy.*

Sure that everything here would hold, he turned back to Kathryn and squeezed her hand. "Go with Mica. He will get you out and to shore. And I will join you there."

Kathryn opened her mouth to protest.

"Please," Patrick cut her off. "I need to know you're safe, and I can't do that right now." Pulling her back into his arms, he pressed his forehead to hers. "I will meet you on the shore, and we will go to town together. I promise."

She pulled back and looked at him. "The town?"

Patrick let out a joyless laugh. "I have to explain to Eustace and the villagers why their castle is filled with dragons." That was a conversation he was sure wouldn't go over well.

Concern crossed Kathryn's face.

"Please," Patrick begged again. "Go with Mica, and I will see you on the other side." He petted her hair back and cupped her face.

Slowly, Kathryn nodded. "All right," she agreed.

Patrick could tell she was not happy with the outcome, but no other answer would do. "Thank you." He kissed her forehead and released her to the waiting mage.

Mica shifted into his grand form and scooped her up.

"Take a deep breath and hold on tight," Patrick coached as Mica limped over to the water's edge with Kathryn clutched in his claws. "You'll be fine, and I'll meet you on the other side."

Kathryn nodded and clung to Mica as they disappeared into the water.

Seeing nothing else he could do here, Patrick shifted back to his greater dragon form and followed his love out. It was time to deal with the village.

Chapter Twelve

TWO FIGHTS WITH A ROGUE DRAGON, FOUR SWIMS across the lake, two runs between the lake and the town, a badly injured dragon with eggs, and a wing dislocated twice made for a very long day. And it wasn't over yet.

The walk back to town was much more leisurely than Patrick had planned. He had tried to get Kathryn to climb on his back so he could carry her, but she refused. Instead, she insisted they walk at a relaxing pace. At first, it had irritated him. He wanted to get back and deal with the town so he could get things done, but now, he was grateful for the time. While Kathryn's fingers slid over his scales, soothing the tension from him, he thought about what he was going to say to the elders. He now had something intelligent to say and wouldn't just blurt out the first thing his tired mind could come up with.

Cresting the short rise that hid the town, the towers of the castle came into view. Patrick stopped to look over the shallow valley. This was his domain—at least, it was for now. The entire area was buzzing with activity. Dragons circled over the castle as the townsfolk scurried around in fear. He didn't see any pitchforks or torches, but Patrick was sure those weren't too far away. Maybe they would attack him when he returned. Maybe they would listen. But that didn't matter. He had chosen this path, and he would walk it proudly.

Taking a deep breath, Patrick reared up on his hind legs, flared his wings, and roared his return. An answer echoed from the castle as the people of the village scampered for cover. Settling back to the ground, he ruffled his wings and set off towards the village with Kathryn at his side. The feel of her hand on his shoulder gave him the strength to face what he needed to do. As long as she accepted him, he didn't care what the villagers thought.

The village was quiet as Patrick and Kathryn made their way to the center of town. Shutters creaked as eyes watched through holes in the wood. The stench of fear was everywhere. Coming to the center of town, Patrick sat back on his haunches and curled his tail around his feet.

Kathryn stroked her hand down his side. "I'll be back," she soothed him and left.

Patrick turned his head to watch her go. Drawing in a deep breath, he let it out slowly. He would stay until someone grew brave enough to face him. His eyes scanned over the homes, catching movement from doors and shutters. There were people here, and they were watching. He just had to wait them out. The sound of a door opening drew his attention, and he shifted to face the brave soul. It was Eustace.

"Stories are told of a time when dragons walked as men," the old man said as he left the safety of his home. "Are you friend or foe?"

Bowing his head, Patrick closed his eyes. At least the old man was willing to talk to him before breaking out the pitchforks. But he would need to shift back to talk with the town elder. Of all the things he had considered while they walked back, standing around naked in the village square hadn't been one of them. He would just have to buck up and hope his dignity could stand the humiliation.

"Friend," Kathryn said as she ran back into the square. Shaking out a sheet, she flung it over Patrick's back.

What a clever girl! Purring his delight, he lowered himself to the ground and shifted. The thin material draped over him, covering him from view. It took a few moments to work the cloth into place, but he stood up with the thing wrapped toga-style around him.

"Thank you." He touched Kathryn's hand before turning to face the old man. The surprise on his face made Patrick smile. "I am not your foe." He looked around as the shutters on the houses were pulled back. Amazed people looked out.

"The dragon has been dealt with," Patrick announced, raising his voice so it echoed through the town square. "He will not bother you again."

A commotion from the castle drew his attention, and he raised his hand out to the line of maidens streaming from the gates. "The maidens he took are safe."

Eustace turned to see the women come racing into the square to greet Kathryn before a few went to find their families. "Are they well?" the town elder asked as doors were flung open and the girls were embraced.

Patrick nodded. "They are well." He glanced around at the happy scene and drew in a deep breath. Here came the tricky part. "My men and I will remain at the castle and work to repair her defenses. We are dragons, but we will offer you no harm." He looked around at the faces of the villagers. It was hard to tell what they were thinking. "We offer you our protection and help until you ask us to leave. At that time, we will make arrangements for a new protector and go without question."

Seeing no answer was coming, he bowed to Eustace. "If you will please forgive me, it has been a long day and there is still much to do before I can rest." Turning, Patrick held his head high and started off towards the castle.

Kathryn glared at Eustace before hurrying to catch up with Patrick. She took his arm and leaned into his side.

Patrick let out a contented sigh and leaned into her. As long as she stood by him, he could handle anything else.

"My Lord Dragon," Eustace called before they could get out of the square.

Stopping, Patrick turned to face him.

"Tell me…" The older man paused as he studied the dragon lord. "The first day you turned the dragon, could you have killed the beast and saved the town from his terror?"

Patrick paused, considering the elder's words. A wrong answer here could change the outcome of the whole day. "Yes," he answered honestly. "My men and I could have killed your dragon on the first day, but the ladies would have paid the price for that action with their lives." He looked at the maidens they had saved. "I stand by my decision to spare the dragon that day."

A rustling of material drew his attention as the first of the girls kissed her family and came to stand next to him. Soon, all the maidens were circled around him.

Eustace let out a laugh. "Well, My Lord Dragon, I will bring this up with the other elders, but I think the maidens have spoken. No one is going to challenge your right to be here and risk the wrath of so many women."

Isn't that the truth! Patrick looked at the ladies around him warily. "No, you don't want to risk that. Unhappy women make for a miserable life."

Most of the girls blushed and looked away from the man they had harassed. The ones he had saved gave him inquisitive looks.

Eustace raised a curious eyebrow. "I see." None of the girls would meet his eye. He let out a laugh. "Go on, My Lord Dragon, you have earned both your rest and our respect. No one here will question your place as lord."

Patrick bowed to him. "Thank you, my good man. My men and I are at your service should ever you need us." With that, he straightened, turned around, and left. The swarm of maidens followed him. After a few steps, he stopped and looked to the ladies. "You are safe now. Feel free to return to your lives."

The woman stared at him expectantly, but they didn't leave.

"Patrick," Kathryn pulled at his arm, gaining his attention, "their things are still at the castle," she reminded him. "Besides, most of these girls lost everything to the dragon."

Enlightenment dawned on Patrick. How dumb could he be? These girls weren't the *only* maidens left in the town, they were the maidens left without *protectors*. It would be shameful to turn them away in their time of need. Not to mention it would be a horrible mark against him in the very fragile beginning. Letting out a sigh, he nodded. "Any who wish to stay at the castle, may."

Joy passed over the ladies' faces as they started off to their new home, giddy.

What had he just agreed to? Patrick turned and followed behind the group of excited girls.

Kathryn pressed into his side. "Plus, if we left, who would take care of *you*?"

Patrick chuckled and wrapped his arm around her shoulders as he walked. "I'm not sure how much more *care* I can handle," he teased.

"We could always go back to the village and let you men fend for yourselves," she huffed at him.

"Anything but that." He squeezed her to his side. "Your leaving is the one thing I could not handle." Letting out a deep sigh, he released his tight hold on her. "Give me a few minutes to send some messages to Prince Kyle, and the rest of the day is yours," he promised. "I will tell you the things you need to know."

Kathryn looked up at him. "But aren't you tired?"

He was sure all the trials of the day were etched into his face. "Exhausted," he admitted. What he truly wanted was a nice long nap, preferably with Kathryn in his arms.

"Then rest," she urged. "I will watch over you as you sleep."

Patrick chuckled. "As you wish, My Lady." Sleep would do him a world of good. And then, he would make sure she understood everything about dragons.

Epilogue

"YOU HAVE A LETTER FROM THE PRINCE." KATHRYN held up the note that had just arrived.

Patrick smiled at her. A single, red scale hung by a thin chain at her throat. His scale. A scale that matched the patch on her shoulder where she had accepted his bonding.

"And what does the prince say, My Lady?" He pushed back from the table where he was working and raised his arms to her.

Kathryn came over and slid into his lap. "I haven't opened it," she said as she cuddled into his embrace. "I didn't think I should. It came with a sizable package."

"Mmm." He kissed her softly and took the letter from her hand. "Then let's see what my brother has sent for us." Breaking the wax seal, he unfolded the paper and read it around her.

After a few quiet moments, Kathryn's curiosity got the better of her. "And?"

Patrick chuckled. "The eggs have hatched. Six healthy dragons—two girls and four boys. The rogue dragon and his family are being transported to a dragon colony away from human society."

"So, he is getting away with murdering all those people?" Kathryn said crossly.

"No." Patrick shook his head as he tried to soothe her. "He will be confined there for his crimes until a proper punishment can be decided. But the extenuating circumstances are being considered. Everything he did was to protect his injured mate. It was, after all, a bolt from the castle's crossbows that nearly killed her."

There was a likely chance that the dragon would be forced into human form and confined to the colony, but he didn't share this bit of information. The fate of the dragon had been a sore subject since Patrick had called the queen in and she had spared the dragon's life. So many people had lost their lives to his reign of terror.

Kathryn let out a deep sigh. "What else does it say?" She turned to look back at the letter.

Patrick kissed her lightly and went back to the letter. "My brother wishes us the best in our bonding and has sent us a present." He looked up at the woman in his lap. "Would you like to go see what it is?"

"Yes." She shifted out of his lap.

Standing, Patrick folded the letter and set it on his table before taking Kathryn's hand. He wrapped it around his arm and guided her out of the castle. There was no telling what his family had sent.

Walking out into the bailey, Patrick looked at the wagon loaded with wrapped parcels. The men had already started to unload it. There were several long bolts of material.

One of the men pulled a roll of it loose. "My Lord," he called. Inside was scarlet red material that had been made into banners for the castle. Embroidered in gold was a dragon rearing up with its wings extended.

Patrick laughed at the image. "My Queen Mother has a sense of humor." He held the banner out for Kathryn to see.

"What do you mean?" she asked. She cocked her head and studied the magnificent piece of work, trying to see what Patrick found amusing.

Grinning, Patrick touched the neck of the dragon. "Each color of dragon has characteristic that separates it from the others. Gold dragons have a bone frill and horns to go with the tufted tail."

"But this one doesn't." Kathryn looked over the image. "This one seems familiar."

"It should. This is a red dragon. They just have the tufted tails," Patrick explained. He snorted out a laugh. "This is me." He rubbed his hand over the stitchwork. "A red dragon, claimed by the golds. Royal by the queen's decree."

Kathryn opened her mouth and shut it again, at a loss for words.

Sensing her inner turmoil, Patrick drew her to his side and kissed he cheek. "This doesn't change anything," he whispered. The royal family had claimed him a long time ago. It was just amusing to see it displayed so prominently by the queen's own hand.

"My Lord," another man called from the other side of the cart.

Patrick turned Kathryn loose and went to see what else had been sent. The men handed down a cradle. Built for a human child, the thing had drag-ons carved in the sides. "Another gift from the Queen Mother." He rubbed his hand down the relief. Again, the dragons had the tufted tails of the reds. "I guess she expects grandchildren soon."

Kathryn blanched and dropped her hand to her flat stomach. "My Lord," she said, distressed.

Patrick came over and took her hand reassuring-ly. "I have not suggested anything to anyone." He kissed her cheek and drew in her scent. The delicate aroma had changed over the last few weeks, and he was almost positive she was with child. But he would wait until she was sure before offering his opinion on the matter. Women in any stage of pregnancy tended to be fickle. He knew. He had spent enough time in the nurseries with nesting females. "We will deal with it when the time comes," he reassured her.

She relaxed under his gentle touch.

Kissing her cheek softly, he turned her around to take her back inside. The men could handle unloading whatever remained in the cart. Yes, they would deal with the future when it came, and he would be the happiest dragon in the land.

Acknowledgements

HERE I FIND MYSELF AT THE END OF ANOTHER BOOK, flabbergasted at the overall response of my fans. When I sat down and started smithing words, I never dreamt that I would ever publish anything, let alone gain such a following for my work. Every day I wake up astounded by this whole thing. This past week I went to a book convention to meet people. I was floored that people were there to meet me. As I sit here writing this, trying not to publicly embarrass myself by bawling in my local coffee shop, I still can't believe it. I just want to thank everyone that has seen fit to pick my novel and dedicate a slice of their life to my words. It doesn't make a difference if you loved it or hated it, everyone is entitled to their opinion and I appreciate that my writing isn't for everyone, what touches me is that you saw merit in it enough to pick it up (though I pray you enjoyed it). Thank you.

I'd like to thank Krys as he puts up with my running off to book conventions when I should be home taking care of things; Karl for understanding

Mommy doesn't always play games on her computer; and my friends at HobbyTown USA in Jackson. You've all been understanding and supportive since I first put pen to paper. Of course, I also have to thank the wonderful team of people at Crimson Tree Publishing for their hard work and sticking with me through this amazing journey. And last, but definitely not least, my family (Mom, Dad, Amanda, Jessica, Grandma, and many more) for listening to me ramble on about these stupid books. God bless the US Troops out defending our country. May you make it home safe. Thank you all.

About the Author

Originally from Ohio, Julie always dreamed of a job in science. Either shooting for the stars or delving into the mysteries of volcanoes. But, life never leads where you expect. In 2007, she moved to Mississippi to be with her significant other.

Now a mother of a hyperactive red headed boy, what time she's not chasing down dirty socks and unsticking toys from the ceiling is spent crafting worlds readers can get lost it. Julie is a self-proclaimed bibliophile and lover of big words. She likes hiking, frogs, interesting earrings, and a plethora of other fun things.

CPSIA information can be obtained at www.ICGtesting.com
Printed in the USA
LVOW06s0430131215

466423LV00005B/86/P